Isolation

Neil Randall

Copyright © 2017 by Neil Randall
Editor: Crooked Cat
All rights reserved.

No part of this book may be used or reproduced in any manner whatsoever without written permission of the author or Crooked Cat except for brief quotations used for promotion or in reviews. This is a work of fiction. Names, characters, and incidents are used fictitiously.

First Black Line Edition, Crooked Cat. 2017

Discover us online:
www.crookedcatbooks.com

Join us on facebook:
www.facebook.com/realcrookedcat

Tweet a photo of yourself holding
this book to **@crookedcatbooks**
and something nice will happen.

For my parents.

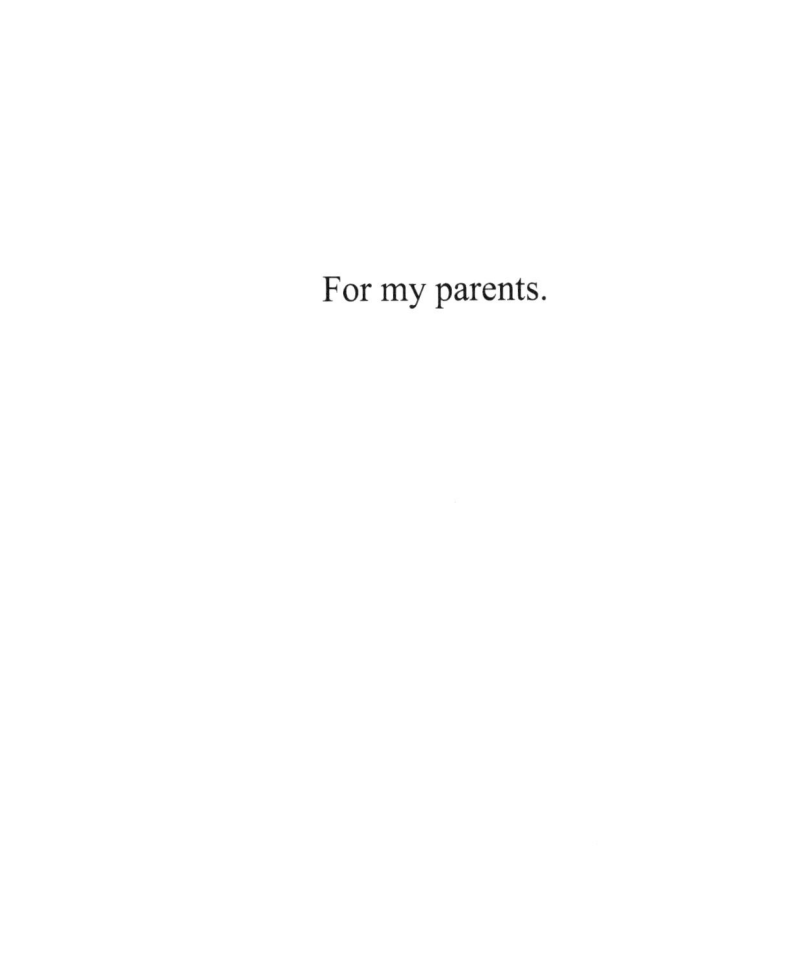

About the Author

Novelist, short story writer and poet, Neil Randall was born in Norfolk, England, in 1975. A keen sportsman, Randall represented his county at football throughout his school and college years, and had trials with several leading English club sides. After attending an elite sport's college, Randall went on to read law at the University of East London. During a gap year he travelled extensively across Central and Eastern Europe and into Russia, places which provide the backdrop for much of his early published work.

He is heavily influenced by classic authors such as Hubert Selby Jnr, John Cheever and Raymond Carver as well as contemporary writers such as Haruki Murakami, Olga Grushin and Paul Auster. He wants to write bizarre compelling stories about normal everyday people and situations, where the reader doesn't know what's coming on the next page.

His shorter fiction and poetry has been published in the United Kingdom, United States, Australia and Canada.

Samples of his writing can be viewed at
www.neilrandall.net and **narandall.blogspot.com**

Acknowledgements

I would like to take the opportunity to thank everyone at Crooked Cat Books for all their hard work in making this book possible. Special thanks goes to my editor Laurence Patterson whose invaluable advice helped make Isolation the dynamite read it is today. I would also like to thank my family and friends for all their support and encouragement over the years.

In terms of background reading and research for Isolation, I am indebted to Tom Mulch's Choctaw Tales and Angie Debo's A History of the Indians of the United States for providing me with an insight into the folkloric tales which I reference in the book.

Finally, I would like to offer thanks to all my writer friends who read early drafts of the novel, making invaluable suggestions along the way. Without your help, I would never have got the book off the ground.

Shani Struthers

Isolation

Chapter One

Monday Morning

As soon as I got to the office I started sorting through the usual correspondence, the interdepartmental reports and agenda updates, circulars from neighbouring borough councils, junk mail from stationery suppliers, letters from MPs, councillors, and disgruntled members of the public. While checking for anything of importance, anything that might require urgent attention, I noticed a slim, plain-white envelope, a very large, unusual envelope, different from the ones I was used to sifting through each morning. To my surprise (despite eight years' continuous service, mine was still a relatively junior position), it had been marked for my attention. *F.A.O. Nigel Barrowman* read the top line of the label, printed in an elegant font – Cambria, I think.

Intrigued, I carefully unsealed the envelope and slid out the contents: a glossy colour photograph, enlarged, of what looked like a luxury hotel room, a room in complete disarray – huge amounts of blood spattered up against the walls, crumpled sheets strewn across the floor, lamps and period furniture overturned, thick drapes torn from curtain rails, a battered crystal chandelier hanging precariously from the ceiling, a dressing-table with a smashed mirror. Most disturbingly of all, on a vast king-sized bed, there lay two bloodied corpses, both young women, white, with tousled, jet-black hair covering their faces, arms splayed at corresponding angles (in what I could only describe as inverted crucifixion poses), naked bodies showcasing a truly sickening array of deep, jagged stab wounds, each woman had a breast sliced off, and a series of intersecting lacerations cut into the stomach which looked to be identical, as if whoever had perpetrated the grisly murders had taken the time to make intricate incisions, like a carver cutting patterns into wood, leaving, perhaps, some kind of message or symbol.

"What?" I picked up the envelope and checked the postmark: London. I turned the photograph over. A date – 06/11/95 – Saturday had been printed on the back. Again, I scrutinised the photograph. Surely it was a prank, a photoshopped image, a bad taste joke. But the more I studied the scene, the more authentic it appeared. There were no telltale signs of cutting or pasting or splicing or smudging or airbrushing. Everything looked natural – well, as natural as a brutal double murder could look, I suppose. And that's when it struck me. If the photograph was genuine, then why had someone sent it to me, why had the envelope been marked for my attention?

The door swung open, making me jump.

"Morning, Nige." My line-manager, Michael, walked into the room. "Good weekend? God, I'm hung-over. Can't take it like I used to. Anything pressing come up? Anything I need to deal with right now?"

"No, no. Only we did receive a rather strange photograph in the post this morning."

"Photograph?" He yawned and rolled his neck. "What kind of photograph?"

"This." I held it up for his perusal. "It was amongst the normal post, marked for my attention."

Michael's handsome, if slightly stubbly, red-eyed face contorted into a worried, disturbed grimace.

"Huh?" He took the picture and studied it at close quarters. "Is this some kind of joke?"

"That's what I thought. But the more I looked at it, the more it seemed, erm...genuine."

"I – I don't know what to say, Nige. This is Ilford, Essex, the Risk and Assessment section of the District Council, not an episode of *Columbo*."

"So what do you think I should do about it, then?"

"Ignore it. Throw it away. It's probably Justin from Street

Works, another one of his pranks, a bloody wind-up. You know what a whizz he is when it comes to computers."

He handed the photograph back.

"Throw it away?"

"Yeah. I'm sure he'll own up before the day's out. And say, Nige, you don't mind holding the fort for a bit, do you? I've got to go straight back out again, got, erm...site meetings, a full diary." A euphemism he often used when taking the rest of the day off. "And if I don't get a strong coffee and a bacon sandwich inside me, I'll be no good to anyone."

"But I've got an appraisal with Mr Mackintosh this afternoon."

"Oh shit, erm...can't be helped," he said reaching for the door handle. "Get the girls on reception to redirect all calls. Catch you later."

"No, no, Ms Braithwaite," I said, switching the telephone from right hand to left, "you can't make a claim against the authority for loss of earnings in this case. Our maintenance section is undertaking essential works to the public highway. We have a duty to ensure that all necessary repair work is, well, if you feel *that* strongly, then I advise you to put the matter to us in writing. Then you—"

She slammed the phone down.

"That's right, Mr Shepherdson, if you put your claim in writing and send it to the address I just gave you, marked for the attention of Michael Oliver, we'll look into the matter and get back to you. No, you can't just give me the details over the telephone. I know it would save a lot of time and effort, and I really am sorry for the inconvenience, but it's procedure. If you want to—"

He slammed the phone down.

"That's not quite the case, Mr Collings. As we outlined in our original letter, the overhanging hedge is on private land. Therefore, if you want to pursue a personal injury claim, you will have to contact the landowner in question. Well, sir, I'm sorry you feel that way. I don't think there's any need for that kind of language. No. I—"

He slammed the phone down.

"So, Nigel," said Mr Mackintosh, Area Coordinator, a severe, craggy-faced man in his late fifties, "where do you see yourself in the next ten to fifteen years?"

"Erm, well, ideally I'd like to continue working in the Risk and Assessment section, adding to my skill base, helping to provide a better standard of customer care." I trailed off having repeated, almost verbatim, the contents of the last set of council directives.

Mackintosh looked me over, in the way a scientist would examine a rare but ultimately useless organism under a microscope.

"I've always admired your dedication – in early, last to leave, rarely if ever sick, monthly reports always delivered to your superiors on time." He gave me that same appraising look again. "Remember, Nigel, not just anyone can work in the public sector. In many ways you were handpicked for your position here. And full-time contracts will soon become a thing of the past."

This only served to unnerve me. In eight years, I'd never heard this scowling, perennially agitated man utter a complimentary word about anyone.

"Granted, you may not be destined for a managerial role, but if you continue to perform in an adequate manner, you'll receive all the benefits associated with a long career in local government."

Just as I was about to leave off for the day, the telephone started to ring.

"Risk and Assessment. How can I help?"

There was a brief pause, what I could only describe as a rustling sound, before a man, whose tone was far too sinister and staged to believe, said:

"Find anything interesting in the post this morning?

Don't worry, Nigel. Plenty more where that came from. This is just the beginning." He slammed the phone down.

"What?"

Whether this was just another part of the prank, the next stage of a distasteful wind-up, Justin's idea of seeing a joke through to the end, I didn't know. Nonetheless I decided to rescue the photograph from the rubbish bin, to keep it as evidence, just in case, to slip it inside my desk drawer, locking it away somewhere safe overnight.

Chapter Two

A trip to the big Sainsbury's in Ilford always filled me with dread. Thoughts of bustling aisles crammed with snarling, sniping shoppers arguing over what they should have for their tea, the price of toilet rolls or baked beans, trolleys being pushed around like demented dodgems, the harsh overhead lighting, customer service announcements crackling through overhead speakers, the incessant bleep-bleep from the check-outs, young mum's manhandling rowdy kids, the queues, the smells of the fish and meat counters, the freshly baked bread, the changes in temperature never failed to unsettle me, inducing something close to one of my old debilitating panic attacks.

Picking up a basket from a stack by the automatic doors, I walked inside the store. Living alone, I tended to buy lots of frozen food, meals-for-one, pizzas, chicken kievs, things I could shove into the oven; things which took little or no preparation time, bar tearing open a cardboard box and piercing the plastic packaging. In theory, therefore, my visits to Sainsbury's should've been relatively painless affairs. Regardless, I always seemed to stumble into an irritating nightmare scenario: a security guard getting into a fist-fight with a shoplifter, an item that wouldn't scan through the check-out properly, precipitating a long delay, interaction with people I found as disconcerting as I did absurd.

Only today, something even stranger happened. Halfway up the dairy aisle, a roly-poly woman didn't so much as slip over as throw herself, swallow-dive fashion to the floor, right by a *Caution Slippery* sign, in a blatant and pretty unspectacular attempt to get some kind of personal injury compensation (and I say unspectacular because she did barely more than slump down on her front). So pathetically transparent was her effort, not one of the many shoppers pushing trolleys up and down the aisle paid her any mind. In fact, no-one, me included, went over and asked if she was okay, if she needed any help. No-one called for a member of staff. We just stepped over her body as she writhed around, moaning and groaning, and carried on our shopping as normal.

The same girl who served me last Friday after work was at the check-out, very pretty, early twenties, with delicate features and soft brown eyes. Last week she asked me lots of questions – "You out on the town tonight?" "Anything nice planned for the weekend?" – things that sounded a little odd and out of place, but things I felt obliged to answer. When I got home and checked my receipt I noticed that many of the things I'd put through the check-out hadn't been scanned, so I hadn't been charged for them.

"Back again?" She smiled, picked up my frozen pizza and scanned it through the till.

"Yeah." I looked at her name-tag: Liz Green.

"Another Monday, another week in the grind."

"They tend to come around quick, don't they?"

It was then I noticed (and it wasn't something I would've been aware of had it not been for last Friday, such was the unceasing volley of bleeps sounding all around me) that Liz was passing my items over the scanner rather than through it. When my shop was totalled up, she only asked for one-pound ninety-nine, the cost of the pizza.

I reached for my wallet, hesitated, was about to say something, but Liz spoke first:

"You know, when a girl does something this stupid to catch a fella's eye, he should really ask her out for a drink."

A wobbly-voiced customer service announcement crackled out of the speakers:

"This week only, one-litre bottles of Robinson's Orange Barely Water – buy one, get one free."

A woman behind me said, "Are you gonna pay for that lot, mate? Other people want to get on, eh?"

I apologised, handed Liz a five-pound note, and shoved my shopping into a carrier bag. When she gave me the change, I was so flustered, so taken aback, I didn't get a chance to say anything to her, so quickly had she started scanning the next customer's shopping, and I found myself shunted away from the check-out, narrowly avoiding a collision with two trolleys.

Back at my modest one-bedroom flat, the top half of an old terraced house that had been knocked into two, I put the shopping away, turned on the oven, and slid my pepperoni pizza inside – gas mark seven, twenty-two minutes. Still a little perplexed by the scene at the supermarket, I walked through to the front room, picked up the remote control and switched on the television, catching the regional news headlines.

"Two unidentified women have been found brutally murdered in a central London hotel room."

Giving a start, I stared at a still photograph of the same murder scene I'd studied earlier this morning, the exact same luxury hotel room, the exact same bloodstains spattered up against the walls, chandelier dangling from the ceiling, overturned furniture and cracked mirror. The only thing missing was the two corpses on the bed.

Deeply disturbed, I slumped down on the settee. I didn't know what to do. Should I call the police? Perhaps ring Michael on his out of hours work phone? Anyone better equipped to deal with the situation than me, anyone who could act in a reasonable, considered manner.

In the end, after pacing up and down the flat, I went through to my bedroom, switched on my computer, accessed the internet, and typed in the BBC's web address.

There it was, the headline on the homepage:

TWO WOMEN HORRIFICALLY MURDERED IN LONDON HOTEL ROOM

The details were a little sketchy. Evidently the bodies had only just been discovered: one of the cleaning staff raised the alarm when she couldn't open the door. As the newsreader had reported, the two young women had yet to be officially identified. The police were now appealing for guests at the hotel over the weekend to come forward with any information. Under the headline was the same photograph of the crime scene I'd seen on the news bulletin. It was the same room featured in the picture I'd received this morning – it was identical, there was no doubt.

Chapter Three

Next morning, after a fitful night's sleep, agonizing over what to do, I went to the local police station to tell them everything I knew.

"Good morning," said a rangy young duty officer. "How can I help?"

I gulped back some saliva, not quite knowing how to broach such a potentially serious matter without coming across as some sort of crackpot.

"Erm, well, look, I know this is going to sound rather odd, but I think I may have some important information, well, not information as such, but evidence, regarding the hotel room killing, the double murder reported on the news yesterday."

"Oh, right." He hesitated and blinked his eyes, as if unsure of how to deal with such a weighty situation. "I'll, erm…just call through to a senior officer."

About a quarter of an hour later, Detective Inspector Kendrick, a slightly haggard-looking man of middle age and medium height, with big bags under his filmy eyes, came out of a back room to meet me.

"Mr Barrowman?" He ushered me over to some chairs in a quiet corner of the reception area. "I understand you've got some information concerning a very serious incident that took place over the weekend."

"That's correct."

"Why don't we sit down and you can tell me all about it?"

In clear, chronological order, I told him about the photograph received at the office yesterday morning, describing the hotel room and corpses in as much detail as I could remember, emphasising the similarity between the crime scene images I'd studied on both the television and the internet.

"And you say the photograph you received is now locked in your desk drawer at work?"

"That's right. I put it there before I left off yesterday afternoon." And I went on to explain that my office was just down the road, walking distance, in fact.

"Okay, Mr Barrowman. If you wouldn't mind waiting here for a few minutes, I'll just have a quick chat with my direct superior, and then we can drive down there."

"It's just through here."

I led Kendrick into the office, switched on the main light, and walked over to my desk. As I took out my keys, I noticed that the drawer had been forced open; the plastic seal around the wooden frame was all broken. When I rummaged around inside, I realised the photograph had disappeared.

"What? But I—"

Taken aback, I have little recollection of what happened next. All I remember is Kendrick's deep monotone voice, a barrage of questions: who has access to the office? who else knew about the photograph?

"Please, try and calm down, Mr Barrowman. That's it. Now, let's look at this from a purely rational point of view. You say you received the letter yesterday, and that it had a London postmark. That's correct, isn't it? So it must've been posted on Friday or Saturday, right?"

I nodded – everything he'd just said sounded reasonable, factual, beyond argument.

"But the murders in the hotel room took place in the early hours of Sunday morning. You couldn't possibly have received a photograph of that particular murder scene, because the incident hadn't even taken place yet."

"But – But I swear to you. The scene depicted in the photograph was identical to the one I saw on the television – the way the blood was spattered up against the wall, the bed sheets, the chandelier. And, please, I'm not some weirdo trying to waste your time. I—" the door swung open.

"Morning, Nige." Michael walked into the room. "How's it…" he trailed off, whether due to Kendrick's presence alone or my visible state of distress was difficult say.

"Ah, here's my line-manager. Michael, I've, erm…been talking to the police about that photograph, the one we received here yesterday morning, the one I showed you."

"What? The prank? The grisly, photo-shopped murder scene?"

While clearly not the answer I wanted, it at least proved I wasn't making the whole thing up, that I wasn't the kind of fantasist I'd just so emphatically started to resemble.

"So you're the other man who saw the photograph, then?"

"That's right."

"Then perhaps we'd better refresh your memory." Kendrick turned to me. "You do have access to the internet here, don't you?"

"Yes. I'll switch my computer on now."

With the three of us crowded around my computer, I accessed the BBC website and clicked onto the story about the murders, so Michael could have a look at the image I'd seen last night.

"Well?" asked Kendrick.

"Erm, yeah, it does look kind of similar, but I couldn't say it was the exact same hotel room – not for certain. I only looked at the photograph for a moment or two. And like I said before, presumed it was a practical joke."

Kendrick asked me a few more questions. All of which I answered with clarity, such was the relief at having the vast majority of my story verified.

"At some stage, Mr Barrowman, we might need you to come into the station and make a full statement. In all likelihood, though, this is just a horrible, horrible coincidence. In all likelihood, someone, like Mr Oliver said, has attempted to play a sick practical joke on you, a joke that has quite incredibly mirrored true life events. The phone call you received at the end of the day would suggest that's the case. With regards to your desk drawer, the fact that someone, most probably a colleague, perhaps the individual who perpetrated the prank, has, in effect broken into the office and damaged council property is something you might want to handle internally, perhaps through your personnel department. For now, I'll put all of the information you've given me into an informal report and pass it on to the team in charge of the investigation."

"No, no, Mrs Morris, from this office we're only responsible for... How long have I worked here? Eight years... No, I don't consider myself to be a jobsworth. Okay, if that's how you feel, by all means, write to the Director. My name's Nigel Barrowman, Technical Assistant, the Risk and Assessment section. Well, I can only hope it won't come to that, to me losing my job, I mean. But you're well within your rights to complain if you think..."

She slammed the phone down.

Blood pounding in my temples I looked down at my desk, at the complaint form, the one I'd been aimlessly doodling on while talking on the telephone, where I'd sketched out something close (or so my memory told me) to the wounds on the dead women's stomachs, the bloody marks that had been scraped across their skin – I was sure of it. Each intersecting line resembled the image that had become embedded in my mind. Only now it was there in front of me. On paper it looked more like an object or an animal than any character or set of characters from an unfamiliar alphabet.

The phone started to ring again.

"Risk and Assessment. How can I help?"

"Is this Mr Nigel Barrowman?"

"That's correct."

"Oh, good. Hope you don't mind me contacting you at work, Mr Barrowman. This regards a, erm…personal matter. And my calling is more than a little, how can I put it? – hopeful than anything else. I'm looking to track down an old acquaintance of yours, someone who, like you, was once an outpatient at St. Peter's hospital."

Mention of St. Peter's completely threw me. However minor or long ago, I didn't like being reminded of my psychiatric treatment by a stranger over the telephone.

"Erm, yes, I was, many years ago now. How can I help? What's this all about?"

"Well, my organisation is trying to track down a member of the same counselling group. And please, rest assured – there's nothing sinister or criminal involved here. We're just concerned about their welfare."

"Who's welfare? Which patient are we talking about?"

"Jeffrey Fuller," he replied, saying a name I hadn't heard, or wanted to hear in many years. "As you probably remember, Jeffrey was a very troubled individual, someone with a lot of, erm…issues, someone not altogether equipped to look after himself. He's been missing for several days now, and it's not like him to just drop out of sight, to not contact his loved ones. So I don't suppose you've heard from him recently, have you, Mr Barrowman? From what we gather, the treatment you undertook was rather unconventional, and it's our understanding that the group as a whole developed quite a strong bond back then."

"No. I'm sorry. I can't help you. I haven't spoken to Jeffrey in over ten years."

Chapter Four

When I got home from work, I hunted out an old photograph album. Inside were pictures of the counselling group the anonymous caller (and in the days that followed, I cursed myself for not having asked for his name) mentioned earlier. As always, it felt strange looking back over this particular chapter of my life, seeing shots of twelve awkward young people dressed all in black and with questionable eighties' haircuts, mainly because I still wasn't sure how I felt about the process as a whole.

To understand why I sought out treatment, I have to go back to my school years, in particular, the months after my final exams. An only child, brought up in a very stuffy, intellectual atmosphere, I spent my formative years surrounded by books. To gain my parents' approval I became an extremely academically minded boy, a voracious reader, a devourer of the written word (to this day, I still read over one hundred books a year). At high school, I dazzled teachers with the breadth and range of my knowledge. There was talk of me going on to Oxford or Cambridge. But when it came to my final examinations, examinations I'd revised incredibly hard for, I cracked under the pressure. I couldn't handle the idea of failure. No sooner had I read the first question on the exam paper than my mind went completely blank. On one extreme occasion I ran out of the hall in tears.

My final results were a disaster. I re-sat and performed even worse the second time around. All of which led to years of depression, anti-social behaviour, a serious eating disorder.

Back then there weren't many specialised support groups or treatment structures in place. After many fruitless, frustrating visits to therapists, I got involved with a group of outpatients at Saint Peter's, taking part in an alternative form of treatment. This was a purely voluntary support group, set up by a young psychotherapist called Dr Rabie, or Ray as he insisted we call him. At the time, he could only have been in his late thirties. An intense, highly intelligent man, he had nevertheless cultivated a laid-back counselling style, where he was particularly adept at getting young people, either hostile to his methods, the whole idea of counselling, or too shy and withdrawn to feel comfortable talking in front of others, into speaking about ourselves and our problems.

The group consisted of myself, Michelle Rouse, Gloria Daniels, Jane Lines, Helen King, Clare Ferguson, Riordan Leach, Cara Clarke, Emma Macpherson, Wendy Lomas, Patricia Gregory and Jeffrey Fuller – all in our late teens, early twenties, all mental patients who hadn't responded to traditional treatments, young people who'd sunk into depression, who'd attempted suicide, self-harmed or turned to drink and drugs, young people with problems whose cause and effect had never really been satisfactorily reconciled.

The counselling sessions themselves lasted for around two hours (although Ray always kept things fluid: if we hit an early impasse, he'd call time on the meeting, if we still had things to contribute, he was happy to let the discussion run to its natural conclusion). In a musty-smelling room in an old public building, we sat and talked about our problems, discussing ways in which we could best function in everyday life. In one session, Helen might talk about her self-harming, how dark moods would often overwhelm her, how she'd sometimes hear voices telling her to take out her frustrations on herself, how relieved she felt when she dug a knife or pair of scissors into her skin. In another session Riordan might talk about the sexual abuse she suffered as a child, how her father and uncle had systematically molested her since the age of ten or eleven, how it had turned her into a nervous, bitter, untrusting wreck, and how she couldn't face up to the world, let alone the idea of a relationship, of being touched or kissed, or even in close proximity to another human being, without drinking copious amounts of strong alcohol.

Or I might try and explain why I'd stopped eating, how food had become the only thing I felt I could control, how pushing a plate of food aside, was, to a very small degree, me reasserting some kind of mastery over my own fate.

Undoubtedly the most volatile and unpredictable member of the group was Jeffrey Fuller. While we were never particularly close, there was, as the only two males in the group, an unspoken solidarity between us, a bond. Even if, in the early sessions, his constant sniping at people as they tried to talk about their problems, his juvenile disruptions, the way he would burp or sigh exasperatedly or blow raspberries, appalled me.

"We're all going to die soon, so what's the point in trying to understand anything?" was his favourite saying, no more than a defence mechanism, a way for him to deal with his own insecurities, the problems he was struggling to handle. It took several weeks before he finally spoke frankly about his personal situation, and why he himself attended the sessions. With a certain sadistic relish, he told us about the morning he attacked his mother with a knife, forcing himself on her, how she pleaded with him to stop, and how cold and indifferent he had felt during and after the incident.

As if ashamed of his disclosure, he went on the offensive again, spitting out a series of caustic, rhetorical questions in his thin, whiny voice:

"Why would a son do something like that to his own mother? Because he's evil? Because he's got the devil inside? Because those pesky voices in his head told him to? Or because he just wanted to get laid?"

After that session, for shock value alone, he often asked me if I'd ever considered raping a woman at knife point, or if I'd ever considered sleeping with my own mother ("if it's good enough for Oedipus, it's good enough for me".). One time, when I'd accepted a lift home in his car, he insisted on cruising the streets, pulling over to the side of the road and propositioning girls, telling them that we were after some action. But he only seemed interested in continuing the conversation if they showed not the slightest bit of interest, and by that I mean, if a girl or group of girls (or young women, I should probably say) responded positively to his advances, he simply drove away. If they got angry and told him to leave them alone, he persisted, became abusive, threatening almost, telling them he wanted to show them what sleeping with a real man was like, how he wanted to screw them until they couldn't walk straight anymore.

I turned a few pages of the photograph album, coming across a picture of Jeffrey and Michelle, in the woods adjoining the hospital grounds, near some picnic tables, a place we often used to congregate, especially in the summer months when the weather was nice. Both had startled, almost angry looks on their faces, and were standing quite a distance apart, unnaturally so, as if this photograph, or perhaps each other's company, was the last place in the world they wanted to be. This concerned me for two reasons: One: because I couldn't remember ever seeing this picture before. Two: because it stirred up a lot of old memories about Michelle, my only ever real, proper, serious girlfriend. Having met during the sessions, we went out for five years, we moved in together. In many ways, we provided each other with a necessary crutch, to help deal with the kinds of everyday issues ordinary people wouldn't find even remotely problematic. But we were far too young and inexperienced to understand the essential truth, the codependent dynamic of our relationship, how our particular conditions could be worsened, our symptoms exacerbated, purely by spending so much time together. After a serious relapse, Michelle's new therapist suggested that we take a break, that perhaps our relationship was holding us both back. That was five years ago. Only without a big argument, a nasty scene, the usual kind of things couples go through when splitting up, I never quite accepted that our time as a couple had ended.

Chapter Five

On evenings like this, when I felt distant and preoccupied and not in any kind of mood to cook, I often went to the fish and chip shop on Goodmayer's Road. It was run by a doddery old Chinese couple, whose constant bickering had been a source of entertainment to customers for years, even if they couldn't understand a word of what husband and wife were saying to each other.

Tonight, when I pushed open the door to all the familiar sensations: the frying fat smell, the television noise from out back, the harsh overhead lighting, I was so distracted, caught up in my own thoughts, I didn't notice that someone was sitting on one of the chairs by the plate-glass window, waiting for their food order. Not until I heard a voice that I recognised from somewhere did I turn my head.

"Fancy seeing you here." Liz Green stood up and walked over. "Must be fate, hey?"

"Erm, yeah, I–I only came here on a whim. Didn't really fancy cooking at this time of night."

"I know what you mean. Not the healthiest of choices, but if you can't be arsed, you can't be arsed." She smiled. "And say, if you ain't ordered yet, do you fancy maybe nipping to the pub down the road? You can buy me that drink, if you want."

"Yeah, okay. But what about your food? Won't it –?"

"Oh, it'll be all right." She waved my words away. "I'll get Mr Wang to shove it in the cabinet, keep it warm for a bit."

In a quiet corner of the almost deserted pub, Liz told me all about her life, how she shared a flat with a friend not too far from mine, how she'd been single for a while now and didn't go out all that much, and how she was going to night school, training to become a counsellor, doing voluntary work for The Samaritans, and helping out at a shelter for the homeless.

"So you live just across the way, then?" she asked. "Springfield Road? Yeah, a few years back, I had a mate who lived down the bottom end, near the butchers. And you work at the council offices?"

"That's right." And I told her about my job in Risk and Assessment, the stupid things I had to deal with each day, all the painful, comi-tragic nonsense, how much stick I got from the general public, how petty people could be sometimes, always trying it on.

"Bloody hell! That's sounds like a bit of a nightmare. Don't know if I'd like all the abuse. Having to get up and go to work is bad enough in itself."

"Yeah, it is."

The first drink, the conversation had passed far too quickly. I was really enjoying myself, and really wanted to ask Liz out on a proper date.

"Could I, erm…have your phone number? Maybe we could go out sometime."

"Course you can. I think I've got a pen in my handbag somewhere. If you've got a scrap of paper floating 'round, we could be in business."

I rummaged through my pockets, pulling out a piece of paper, the complaint form I'd been doodling on at work earlier.

"Hold up." Liz pointed to the pattern I'd sketched. "What's that all about?"

"Oh, nothing." I let her take the piece of paper from my hand. "Just a form from work. I'm always doodling rubbish when I'm bored."

Liz didn't say anything; she was too busy studying the pattern or symbol or whatever it was.

"What is it?" I asked.

"Well." She lifted her head, "I might be wrong, but this looks familiar."

"Familiar? How?"

"Looks like a horned owl, the kind Native Americans feared. Used to read loads of that kinda folklore stuff at school, and if I'm not mistaken, that crescent moon shape is the head, then you've got the wings and the body"– she gestured to the sheet of paper again – "it symbolises death or bad luck or something."

"Horned owl? Death?" An image of the hotel room, the same bloodied patterns scraped across the dead women's skin flashed before my eyes. "Really?"

"Yeah, no bullshit. And you say you just doodled this at work, at random? Bit worrying that." She giggled and nudged my elbow. "Might've been the horned owl channelling its dark powers through your hand. Might be a message from the fiery pits of hell or wherever."

"Oh, I don't know about that. I was talking to a snooty old woman who'd tripped on a broken cellar light. Maybe I unconsciously wanted to send her to the fiery pits of hell."

"Ha!" Liz took a sip of her gin and tonic. "Maybe I've got it wrong, though. Maybe it's got nothing to do with anything of the sort. But I always felt proper outraged about how the Native American, the true indigenous peoples were treated, how they were forced offa their own land, 'cause they had such a spiritual connection to nature, to all living things, a kinda mystical wisdom, if you like, one that went far deeper than most religions ever do. That's why I remember the image of the horned owl. It sorta stuck in my mind."

"And you're sure it symbolises death, that it's an omen or portent or whatever?"

"Well, yeah, I think so." She placed the piece of paper on the table. "I ain't freaked you out, have I?"

"No, no, it's just odd, that's all. I don't know why I'd just sketch out something like that."

"What? Are you all superstitious? Is that what you mean?"

"Not superstitious as such, but I do believe certain things happen for reasons we might not be able to comprehend."

Liz looked very serious again. "Are you free Saturday?"

"Saturday? Erm, yeah, I think so."

"Well, if you really wanna find out more about that symbol, we could always go to Portobello Road Market. I know a fella down there, a friend of the family, he's got a stall, sells all sorts of trinkets, antiques, that kinda thing, bangs out loads of Native American woodcarvings. I bet he'd know all about that owl, bet he'd be able to put you in the picture all right."

Chapter Six

Halfway to work I remembered the training course I was scheduled to attend in Stratford, a pointless two-hour exercise about the latest spreadsheet package. As I walked to the bus-stop, I thought back to yesterday evening, the sheer randomness of bumping into Liz like that, how well we'd got on, how comfortable I felt with her. But more than anything, I thought about the horned owl symbol. What did it really mean? Was it just another unsettling coincidence? Or was there some kind of connection with the photograph of the murder scene?

"Ah!" someone cried out, disturbing my thoughts.

I looked up, towards the crowded bus-stop. To my astonishment I saw the same roly-poly woman I'd seen in the supermarket two days ago, stumbling off the pavement, bundling her way into the side of the bus as it slowed almost to a stop, and tumbling to the pavement. Once again, the ordinary, everyday people in the immediate vicinity paid her little or no mind. Not until the bus driver, a stout, broad-shouldered man, disembarked and started berating her did anything like an incident with bystanders looking on take place.

"Not again!" he shouted. "Third bloody time in a fortnight you've tried to pull this stunt on me. And it stops now, you hear? If I you do your dying swan act again, I'll report you to the bloody police."

"Hi, Nige," said Michael. "Good training course this morning? Get much out of it?"

I didn't answer. Crouched by my desk was a man I'd never seen before, a quite old man, mid- to late sixties, wearing faded blue overalls, in the throes of repairing or replacing my desk drawer.

"Morning," I said, cringing at the mess he'd made of my supremely well-ordered work space – rusty tools strewn across the desktop, pen pot and staple gun overturned, coffee stains on a report I printed off yesterday. "What do you think happened?" I asked, even though it was a stupid question with an obvious answer.

"Well." He hauled himself up to his feet, joints creaking, using the desk for leverage. "Looks like someone took a screwdriver, not a big 'un, mind – these drawers are pretty flimsy, don't take much forcing open – shoved it in the gap there, and busted the lock off. New one on me, this, though. I mean, who'd wanna break into someone's desk drawer, here, in a bloody council office? Makes me wonder what you had stored away in there, old son. Weren't hiding something you shouldn't have been, were you?"

"Oh, and Nige, I nearly forgot." Michael started gathering up his things. "Balls in a bag and all that. But that policeman chap, the one who called in the other day, Detective Inspector Hendrick, Kendrick, whatever his name is, rang earlier, wants you to call him back, soon as you can, sounded pretty urgent. Here's his number."

I glanced up at the clock above the main door: half-past three, almost to the minute, around four hours after I'd arrived following the predictably boring and pointless presentation.

"Oh right." I tried to mask my irritation, even though I was seething inside – how could someone forget something like that?

I waited until Michael had left the office, citing his usual fictitious series of site visits, before returning Kendrick's call.

"Ah, Mr Barrowman, I've been waiting to hear back from you. A few things have come up, re: the incident in the central London hotel room, and we really need to speak to you again, as soon as possible."

I told him that I was currently at work, but if it really was that important, I could organise some cover, have my calls redirected to another department, and drop by the station right away.

"If you could, we'd be most grateful. One of the officers involved with the investigation is here at present, so it would save a lot of time if you could call in now."

"Mr Barrowman." Kendrick led me into a grey-walled interview room. "This is Senior Detective Inspector Terry Watson." He gestured to a thick-set, ruddy-faced man in his early fifties. "As I said over the telephone, we need to ask you a few more questions about the photograph received at your office on Monday."

The two policemen sat one side of a table, me the other.

"As ascertained at our first meeting, the envelope in which the photograph was sent had a London postmark – you remember that clearly, don't you?"

"That's right."

"Therefore, we assumed that the whole thing must've been a coincidence, a prank, a sick joke, because the incident actually took place on the Sunday. However, when receiving your informal statement, the team investigating the murders flagged up a few very striking similarities. None more so than the positions in which the victims were lying on the bed, and the wounds inflicted to their bodies."

"Hang on. So you're saying that the corpses in the hotel room were in the exact same positions as I described, and with the exact same markings?"

Reluctantly, or so it appeared to me at the time, Kendrick nodded.

"That being the case," said Watson, taking over, "we have to accept that the envelope in which you received the photograph may not have been the envelope in which it was delivered. Put simply: whoever sent it wanted us to believe that it couldn't possibly have been a photograph of the actual crime scene, because, as aforementioned, the murders hadn't taken place yet. Why or to what purpose remains to be seen." He picked a pen and a leather-bound notebook up from off the table. "As a matter of course, therefore, we need to ask you a few more questions. Firstly, and please don't take this the wrong way – it's merely procedure, a way of eliminating you from our inquiries – but where were you in the early hours of Sunday morning?"

"In bed," I almost shouted, so shaken was I, not just by the disclosure regarding the photographs, but by the inference, in having gone from conscientious citizen helping police with their inquiries to potential murder suspect.

"I thought you'd say that." Watson smiled blankly. "But you live alone, don't you? Not married, no kids. So is there anyone who can verify that you were at home around the time the incident took place?"

"No. No there isn't."

"And what did you do earlier in the day?"

It was then I started to panic, becoming flustered, tearful almost, unable to form anything resembling a coherent sentence, let alone a response.

"Please, Mr Barrowman, calm down," said Watson. "And rest assured. You're not, at this early stage, a suspect in the murders. Like I said, we just need to ask you a few standard questions to eliminate you from our inquiries."

With a little further firm prompting, I managed to regulate my breathing, and inform him of my movements on the Sunday – how I got the papers, had a late, lazy breakfast, did some washing and ironing in preparation for the working week, had something to eat, a ready-meal, watched a woeful Bruce Willis film, went to bed early and read a few chapters of a book.

"That's fine, Mr Barrowman, thank you. Now, I'd like to clear up a few things with regards to the photograph."

To his very specific questions, I relayed everything I'd told Kendrick previously, describing the scene in as much detail as I could remember.

"Right, good. Next, I'd like to ask you about your workplace, your colleagues, the people you suspected of sending the photograph in the first place, the layout of the building, who has access to your office, the keys to the main building itself, and the damage done to the desk drawer."

All of this I told him, adding:

"Oh, and the desk drawer has just been repaired."

They exchanged a sharp sideways glance.

"That's unfortunate," said Watson, a hint of admonishment in his voice (clearly directed at Kendrick). "Now we won't be able to check for any fingerprints and suchlike."

A few moments of prickly silence passed.

Watson coughed and cleared his throat. "And has anything else unusual happened these last few days?"

"Erm," I hesitated, unsure if I should to tell him about the horned owl symbol and the anonymous phone call regarding Jeffrey Fuller. "No, not really," I said, fearful of coming across as some kind of unbalanced, conspiracy theorist. "I mean, in my line of work, I receive lots of strange phone calls, most of them abusive, but nothing like the photograph."

"Okay. In far more general terms, then, have you any idea why someone would want to send you such a grisly picture? Have you ever been in trouble with the police before? Have you ever knowingly consorted with criminal elements?"

All of which I answered in the negative – because it was, to the best of my knowledge, true.

As the interview drew to a close, I couldn't help asking a question of my own:

"And the two women in the hotel room, have they been identified?"

"Not as yet," said Watson. "Hopefully, in the next twenty-four hours, we can make a formal announcement to the press, appealing for any information. Hopefully, the crime scene will yield enough physical evidence to give us a chance of nailing this sick bastard or bastards in super quick time."

Chapter Seven

As I rushed home, my mind plagued by all kinds of worrying thoughts, I stumbled upon a man and a woman arguing heatedly, making angry gestures and swearing a lot. In an instant, I recognised the woman's voice.

"Liz?"

She swung round. In the orangey street light glow I could see that her eyes were red and puffy from crying.

"Who's this twat?" said a stocky man with a chewed-up face – adding with a derisive sneer: "Your new fella, the posh wanker you were telling me 'bout? Ha!"

"None of your business." Liz turned back to him. "Now why don't you just leave me alone, eh? I don't want all this hassle every time I bump into you. It's not fair. I just wanna get on with my life."

As if I wasn't there, they started to argue again, to shout at each other.

"Look." I stepped in between them. "I don't know what's going on here. I don't even know who you are. But Liz clearly doesn't want to talk to you anymore."

The man (name, as I later discovered: Scott, Liz's psychotic, career criminal of an ex-boyfriend) looked me over, his cold, dark, brutal eyes narrowing in his head.

"Are you having a pop, pal? 'Cause if you are I'll—"

"No!" Liz grabbed my arm and dragged me away. "Just leave it, Scott. If you lay a hand on either of us I'll get Mick involved, and you know what that means."

Her words had a clear and visible effect. Scott took a step backward, a small step in physical terms, but a significant one in relation to the present situation. All of which left me wondering: who was Mick? And why did the mere mention of his name have the power to stop a dangerous-looking individual like Scott Richmond in his tracks?

"All right, all right," he said. "I'm off. You and matey boy can go fuck yourselves."

I put two cups of tea on the kitchen table.

"Thanks." Liz gave me a grateful look. "Sorry about all of that. Scott is such a pain in the arse. I should never have got involved with him." She sighed deeply. "Let's just say he's a proper dickhead, the biggest mistake of my life, and leave it at that."

I nodded and took the chair opposite, sensing that Liz meant what she said; that she didn't want to talk about it.

"So." She leaned forward slightly, cradling the cup with her hands. "You thought any more about that Native American thing we checked out last night?"

I hesitated, not knowing if I should tell her about everything that had happened over the last few days. For one, it might make me look like a weirdo, an unbalanced individual wasting police time. On the other hand, Liz had such an open, easy, natural way about her, to have withheld anything, to not have told her the truth wouldn't have seemed right.

"Not really. Something unusual came up at work."

"Unusual? How'd you mean?"

"Well, you're not going to believe this, but it's absolutely true." And I told her the whole story about the photograph, the bodies in the hotel room, and today's formal interview with the police.

"Really? Straight up? 'Cause I remember seeing that murder story on the news the other night."

"Me too. That's when I started to freak out, because the photograph on all the bulletins showed the exact same hotel room in the picture sent in the post."

"Bloody hell! Life's never dull when you're around, is it?" She chuckled and shook her head. "Supernatural symbols, murder mysteries, can't wait for Saturday now, can't wait to get down to Portobello, can't wait to find out what that horned owl thing is all about."

Chapter Eight

Next morning when I got to work I knew it was going to be another far from ordinary day: three police cars were parked directly outside the main building.

"What's your name, please, sir?" asked the policeman stationed by the door. "And which department do you work in?"

When I told him, he checked my details against a list affixed to a clipboard.

"Oh, right...Mr Barrowman." He ran a line through my name. "You've already given a statement, haven't you?" I nodded. "At present, Detective Inspector Kendrick is in your office. I think he'd like to have a quick chat with you before your colleagues arrive."

I found Kendrick and Watson deep in conversation, standing by my desk, which they'd clearly requisitioned.

"Ah, good morning, Mr Barrowman," said Kendrick, with disarming breeziness, considering the situation. "As you've probably gathered, we're here to follow-up on the information you gave us yesterday. We need to speak to your colleagues, to try and find out what happened to the photograph taken from your desk drawer. Unfortunately, the crime scene at the hotel didn't yield anything like the kind of physical evidence we were hoping for. In light of that, we feel it best to pursue this line of inquiry as vigorously as possible."

Watson took a sip from a plastic cup of instant coffee.

"You always come into work this early, do you, Mr Barrowman?"

"Yes I do. I like to get all my paperwork done while the office is quiet. Some days, the phones can be madness."

He nodded his head a few times, as if digesting what I'd

just said.

"Very strange set of circumstances. I don't mind telling you, we're completely baffled by this link, why anyone involved with the killings would send a photograph of the scene here, to a council office, marked for your attention."

I didn't really like the way he said that – his voice, or so it sounded to me at time, contained a hint of accusation.

"This morning, in the main conference room, we intend to interview each and every employee. See if we can't get to the bottom of this. See if we can't find out who took that photograph."

"Not to freak you out, Nige," said Michael, just after he'd been interviewed, "but those detectives did ask a hell of a lot of questions about you."

"Me? Why did they ask questions about me? I...what sort of questions?"

"Oh, just general stuff – how long you've worked here, what kind of character you are, have you ever acted erratically, has there been any unusual incidents involving you in the past? – stuff like that."

"But – But what I have done bar sorting through the Monday morning post?"

"Just letting you know, don't shoot the messenger. Only I got the distinct impression that the police are clasping at straws."

This troubled me so much, I don't think I even acknowledged Michael when he made his usual excuse to leave off early. I don't think I even noticed him walking out of the door. Only when the phone started to ring did I shake myself from this deep, involving mental fugue.

"Risk and Assessment, how can I help?"

There was a relatively long pause before a well-spoken, almost theatrical-sounding old woman blurted out:

"It's happened again."

"I'm sorry. What's happened again?"

"Those awful street dogs have fouled the pavement outside my property. For the umpteenth time I've had the misfortune of walking their heinous-smelling excrement into my house, ruining my lovely carpets."

"I'm sorry to hear that, madam, really I am. But I'm afraid you've been put through to the Risk and Assessment section in error, not Environmental Health. I deal with potential liability claims against the Local Authority, not with dogs fouling the pavements."

"There's been no mistake, young man – no mistake at all. I specifically requested your department because I would like to make a claim for damages."

"I see. Well, if that's the case you'll still have to contact the Environmental Health section. From this office, we only deal with claims regarding the actual fabric of the road – potholes, uneven pavements, subsidence, drainage issues."

She didn't respond right away, all I could hear were her deep, wheezing breaths, before she hissed:

"You really are a horrible little man, aren't you?"

"I – I beg your pardon."

"Sitting in your ivory tower, hiding away from the real world. I've dealt with your kind before..." as she launched into the usual kind of rant, I moved the receiver away from my ear, hoping she'd soon run out of steam, so I could apologise for the inconvenience, and give her the contact details of the relevant department.

Only she didn't stop.

Her words became angrier, far more abusive, until the entire tone of her voice had changed, until it sounded as if I was listening to a completely different person, of a different sex, with a snarling, rasping voice, until he was calling me out direct, threatening me:

"Time's up, Barrowman. Now you're going to pay for all the horrible things that you've done."

I slammed the phone down.

"Mr Barrowman."

I turned to see Kendrick walking up the corridor.

"About to leave off?"

"That's right."

"Very conscientious, aren't you? First in, last to leave. You're a boss' dream."

Almost involuntarily, I gave a slight, self-deprecatory shrug.

"I'm glad I caught you, though," he said, loosening his tie. "Today's been an interesting, if not wholly productive exercise."

"How'd you mean?"

"Well, no one came forward and admitted to photoshopping a picture and sending it to you as a prank, nor, unsurprisingly, to breaking into your desk and removing it from the drawer. Over the next few days, we're going to run checks on all the computers in the building. See if anyone has left any cyber traces as it were. But we're not holding out much hope."

"So you don't think anyone who works here is responsible, then?"

"I didn't say that, Mr Barrowman. We'll just have to see how things pan out." He half smiled and stared at me for a moment or two longer than was really necessary – no matter what the circumstances. "If anything else unusual happens, make sure you contact us straight away. Okay?" Again he held my stare, as if he knew that unusual things had been happening ever since I received that photograph. "Enjoy the rest of your evening. We'll no doubt be in touch soon."

As I rummaged around my pockets for the front door keys, someone shouted what sounded like my name. I turned to see who it was, only to be hit straight in the face, with what I have no idea – it could easily have been a fist, a shovel, an iron bar or a baseball bat. Dazed, I collapsed to the pavement, just as a well-directed kick thudded into my ribs. After that, everything was such a blur – the blows, the panting breath – I had no idea who attacked me or how many of them there were. The only thing I retain with any clarity was the veiled Asian woman who rushed past with a young child, the way she turned and stared at me writhing around on the floor, the way her eyes contained not a trace of compassion or concern, just mild curiosity, and how she went on her way without coming to my aid, without so much as a word in my attacker or attackers' direction.

Chapter Nine

The radio alarm woke me up, an Oasis song, all pounding drums, thumping guitars and soaring vocals. Hauling my sore, aching, still fully clothed self up off the bed, I stumbled through to the bathroom, pulled the light cord, and looked at myself in the mirror. Amazingly, considering the weight of the first blow to the face, there was relatively little bruising, little visible traces of the attack, bar a rivulet of dried blood encrusted to my top lip. Most of the damage, the reason I was in such intense discomfort, must've been done internally. Rolling up my jumper, I fingered my bruised ribs, grimaced, had to reach for the sink for support, such was the brutal intensity of the shooting pains.

"Scott Richmond," I looked up and said to my bleary-eyed reflection.

After a very brief, very uncomfortable shower, I towelled myself down as carefully as possible, went back through to the bedroom and put on some clean clothes. As I struggled with socks and pants, trousers and shirt, I didn't know what to do for the best. If I had been attacked by a jealous ex-boyfriend then I didn't really want to go to the police, certainly not without speaking to Liz first, because I had no idea what the ramifications would be, and didn't want to cause her any unnecessary aggravation.

At work, I began sorting through the morning mail, every now and then shifting in my chair, right then left, stretching, rolling my neck, searching for the most comfortable angle, testing out my pain threshold. Towards the bottom of the pile of correspondence, I found another envelope marked for my attention, a regulation brown envelope with a neat label printed in the same elegant font as before: Cambria. Shocked as I was curious, I peeled the sticky adhesive flap open and slipped out the contents, a newspaper clipping of some kind. *Obituary. Doctor Lawrence "Ray" Rabie.* My Doctor Rabie, from the counselling sessions all those years ago. Still, it took a while for me to reconcile this with the black and white photograph accompanying the article – he looked so much older, was almost bald, clean-shaven, and dressed in a sober suit and tie.

I then began to read in earnest:

Obituary

In the early hours of the morning, renowned psychotherapist, Doctor Lawrence Rabie, died at his home at the age of forty-nine. Educated at Oxbridge, Rabie was considered one of the finest specialists in his field, championing new and innovative techniques in dealing with mental illness in young people. Like many physicians of his generation, Rabie was a devotee of Freud and Jung, of delving deep into the unconscious mind to unlock the key to the development of mental illnesses in patients. In both the academic and practical fields, Rabie rigorously studied the impact of socialisation and environment on the adolescent mind, in confronting problems direct, removing the mental tumour as he wrote in his one and only full-length treatise, the best-selling Is There Any Such Thing As a Feeling? Here Rabie's treatment differed from his peers, for he felt that only by empathetic transference, by sharing their problems, their secret insecurities and worst fears within a tight-knit group environment, would patients be able to overcome their mental health problems. In a 1987 interview with New Therapies Magazine, Rabie explained his theory: 'Over many years of practical research, I've found that young pubescent and post-pubescent people, the thirteen to twenty-one age group, say, need to connect with others with similar problems, just so they don't feel isolated, as if they are suffering alone, as if they are the only ones to ever feel the way they are at that moment feeling. It really is as simple as a problem shared, a problem halved. Although, like all simple things in life, implementation can often prove incredibly difficult'. After many successes in the field, and the publication of the above mentioned book, Rabie's professional stock couldn't have been higher. In the late 1980s he was very active on the lecture circuit, a hugely in-demand (and hugely well remunerated) public speaker, especially in North America and Canada. That's not to say his career was without its problems. One of the first therapists to champion anti-psychotic medication for adolescent patients, Rabie's later techniques, which relied heavily on the administration of these powerful mood-stabilising drugs, garnered considerable controversy. Hardly surprising when one considers a spate of medication–related suicides in the mid- to late eighties, and the removal of many of the drugs Rabie recommended from the market. He is, and will remain, therefore, a figure that divides public opinion. A scientist possessed of a brilliant mind, no doubt, but someone who will always be associated with perhaps treating his patients as laboratory test subjects rather than vulnerable human beings.

He is survived by his wife, Jorell, and their two grown-up children, Winston and Pippa.

Doctor Lawrence Rabie, clueless, bungling, incompetent headshrinker responsible for damaging many a perfectly sane youngster, born 26th April 1939; died 10th November 1995.

The door swung open.

"Bloody hell!" said Michael. "You heard the news yet, Nige?"

"News? What news?"

"The police have just released the names of those two young women, the ones who were murdered in that hotel room."

"Really? Who were they?"

Michael couldn't remember – he'd only just heard the news on the radio on his way in.

Desperate to find out, I accessed the internet and typed in the BBC webpage address. The main headline was:

HOTEL MURDER VICTIMS NAMED

Below it:

This morning, police have identified the two young women killed last weekend in a central London hotel. Helen King and Riordan Leach...

I gasped, stopped reading, and glanced at the two passport-like photographs of the victims – it was like staring at one of the pictures from my photograph album at home.

In the disorientating moments that followed, I must've had some kind of panic attack, for Michael rushed around his desk and put his hand on my shoulder.

"Nige! Are you all right?"

I'm not really sure what happened next: a glass of water, a few work colleagues looking on concernedly, a phone call to the police, Kendrick leading me out of the main building, telling me to calm down, that it was essential that I told him everything I knew.

"Okay, Mr Barrowman," said Watson. "Don't worry if there are certain things you didn't tell us before. We understand completely. Events have moved at such a hectic and inexplicable pace. But, to try and piece the jigsaw together, we need you to fill in all the gaps. Start with the photograph again, and work your way forward, day by day, step by step."

We were sitting in the same interview room as before. Far more in control of my mind now, I told them absolutely everything, no matter how far-fetched, tenuous or ridiculous it sounded: the horned owl symbol, the mysterious phone call regarding the whereabouts of Jeffrey Fuller, last night's attack outside my flat (and whether it was related to Liz or not) culminating with the obituary; the clipping and envelope of which were now in their possession.

"Right, thank you, Mr Barrowman. We'd like you tell us a little bit more about the group therapy sessions now. We've got the names of all your fellow patients, the therapist who oversaw the treatment, but could you explain what you actually did, the content and nature of your discussions?"

"I'll try." I rubbed a forefinger over lips dry and flaky from talking so much. "At first, it was all a bit awkward, contrived, uncomfortable – this incredibly enthusiastic, earnest, trendy young therapist asking us to do all these cringe worthy exercises."

"Cringe worthy?" said Kendrick. "How do you mean?"

"Well, it was very New Age, hippyish, I suppose you'd say. Often we'd be instructed to pair off, sit cross-legged, facing each other, and talk about our lives, our conditions, to explain why we harmed ourselves or refused to eat, became violent and unreasonable, got drunk and took drugs. If our conversations reached an impasse, Rabie would come over and encourage us to shout and scream, to beat our chests if need be, to try and ease the psychic blockage, so he said. All of which, as you can no doubt imagine, made us – twelve strangers, young people not best-equipped to deal with any kind of social situation – feel incredibly stupid. But, after time, it did have some effect; we did feel much more at ease with each other. And after a few weeks, we were really opening up, talking about our problems. Only…"

"Only what?"

"Only the whole thing became too insular, too intense. The only people we felt comfortable talking to were each other. At home, and I know this was the case with the others, because we often talked about it, we still had problems connecting with our parents. We still resented them, for whatever reason. Put simply: none of us took our new found confidence out into the everyday world. It was only inside the circle that we were able to function in the way Rabie hoped we would elsewhere."

"And was he aware of this?" asked Watson, "–the therapist, I mean."

"Of course. He thought it was a natural stage in our progression. And it became the main focus of our sessions. To counter 'the wall', as he called it, he encouraged us to paint, write stories and poems, dance, stand up in front of each other, recite, perform. It all got very, erm…I was going to say theatrical, but maybe farcical would be a better word. Because I don't think many of us could take all that stuff seriously."

"And you said that Jeffrey Fuller, the subject of the unexpected phone call to your office, was a very volatile, disruptive individual."

"That's right. Jeffrey was deeply troubled. As I mentioned earlier, he'd either raped, or attempted to rape his own mother. Understandably, he had a lot of issues, bottled up guilt, shame, rage, associated with this, and it often manifested itself in the group."

"And was he ever violent?"

"Erm, only once…" I went on to tell them about the time Fuller, completely unprovoked, with little or no warning, attacked Michelle, dragging her to the floor, pulling her hair, pummelling her with his puny fists. It only lasted for a handful of seconds. As Fuller was not a particularly big or strong youth, both myself and Dr Rabie easily subdued him.

"And Michelle Rouse was your girlfriend at the time?"

"Not at the time as such," I corrected him. "We didn't really start going out properly until after the group sessions ended, due to funding issues. Even though we were very close, very tactile within the group – which, I should probably add, Doctor Rabie also encouraged."

"He encouraged you to be tactile?"

"Yes. To hold hands, to hug each other. He felt it helped to put us at ease."

"And how did Rabie and Fuller interact? What kind of relationship did they have? The final lines of the mocked-up, counterfeit obituary suggest that whoever put it together harboured a lot of animosity towards the doctor."

I gave this some thought before answering, because, looking back, I found the dynamic between Dr Fuller and the rest of the group hard to explain. He was so full-on, so incredibly interested in everything we said or did, to an almost suffocating degree. And with regards to Fuller, he resented everyone, was so angry.

"Well, erm…there was a little friction between them, a few heated arguments. But Fuller was like that all the time, always snapping and snarling, picking a fight, always dredging up stuff from past sessions."

"Enough to do a man serious physical harm, to bear a grudge all this time?"

Again I hesitated, fully understanding the inference.

"That I couldn't say."

Watson took some papers out of a folder.

"Right, Mr Barrowman, please don't be alarmed by what we're going to discuss next, but after talking to your colleagues yesterday, we thought it would be prudent to check your medical records."

"My medical records?"

"That's right." He studied the top sheet in front of him. "Now, you've told us about your early mental health problems – the exam pressures, your eating disorder – but it also says here that over the years you were prescribed several different anti-psychotic drugs, with differing results, that you often became delusional."

"That's correct." I shifted uncomfortably. "After the counselling sessions ended, I went through a bit of strange directionless period. My parents didn't really know what to do with me. I had long spells on the dole, where all I did was see Michelle. The original medication I was prescribed only made me feel lethargic. That's why I requested to be taken off it. After that, I had a bit more energy, a bit more ambition, I suppose you'd say. I found employment – nothing spectacular, but jobs which made me feel a lot more confident in myself, part of society as a whole."

"But you did have other problems, didn't you, Mr Barrowman?"

Two firm knocks sounded against the door. A moment later, the handle turned and a uniformed officer poked his head into the room.

"Sir," he panted, clearly out of breath, "a body, a body has been found, all cut up, found when our lads called 'round to that house in Norfolk, a body belonging to Doctor Lawrence Rabie."

Chapter Ten

By the time the police had escorted me home, details of Doctor Rabie's grisly murder had started to break. Desperate for further information, I scoured the internet, going from one news site to the next, trying to learn as much about the killing and crime scene as I possibly could. I wanted to know exactly what 'macabre stab wounds' meant, if the killer had carved the same symbol into Rabie's skin as the other two victims. What horrified me most, though, was the fact that the obituary had been sent in yesterday's post (of this there could be no doubt: on this occasion the date and London postmark were plain to see). Therefore, whoever had sent it – and at this stage both Watson and Kendrick were working on the assumption that it was the murderer – had been planning to kill Rabie shortly afterwards. A clear expression of premeditation.

As a precaution, Kendrick had arranged for a police presence to remain outside my flat overnight. Regardless, it didn't really put my mind at rest; it didn't make me feel any less exposed.

Only when Liz called round (and she had quite a job persuading the police that she was my girlfriend) did I feel at ease.

"What's going on?" She met me in the hallway. "Why you got bloody policemen guarding your flat?"

I told her all about the obituary.

"So this doctor fella, you were one of his past patients?"

"That's right."

Wary of revealing the whole truth, something so personal, I nevertheless told her about my troubles as a teenager, the distant relationship I had with my parents, the exam pressure that go the better of me, my problems with food, and how I ended up needing counselling.

"I hate to lay all this stuff on you, Liz. You probably think I'm a bit of nutcase now. You probably want to run a mile."

"No I don't." She took hold of my hands. "None of this is your fault. I'm not going anywhere. And besides..." she trailed off, reached out and touched the side of my face. "Are you okay? Your face, you look a little – a little, I don't know, like you've been in the wars or something."

With even more reluctance, I told her about the incident last night, about the attack outside my own front door, how I wasn't sure if it was connected to the photograph and the murders or whether it had something to do with her ex-boyfriend.

"Bastard!"

"What? So you think it was Scott, then?"

She looked at me with such anguish in her eyes, I felt like reaching out and drawing her close.

"Wouldn't be the first time. Shit! I feel terrible. With all this other stuff going on in your life, now you've got a cretin like him attacking you. I'm so sorry, Nigel. I'll have a word with a few of my dad's old mates...should've done it the other night, should've known. Don't worry. I'll make sure Scott never troubles you again."

"Look, don't get upset. Some things are worth getting a punch in the face for. And as regards the other stuff, I don't know what to make of it, nor do the police. I just can't understand why I'm involved. I'm just a normal, average guy who works for the council."

We sat at the kitchen table and discussed everything that had happened, breaking things down, rationalising events, exploring each and every likely explanation.

"So do you think this has got something to do with the horned owl, all that Native American stuff we talked about the other night?"

"I'm not sure. But if Doctor Rabie, as the news reports suggest, had been mutilated in the same way as the two women in the hotel room, then chances are he's had the same symbol carved across his skin. I mean, I saw the other bodies. I saw how much time and care must've gone into scraping that horned owl symbol across their stomachs. If someone was going to go to that much trouble, then it must mean something."

Liz agreed. "This is getting darker by the minute. Reckon we should definitely go and see my mate down Portobello tomorrow. What he don't know about all this Native American folklore business ain't worth knowing. Bet—"

"But I'm not sure if the police will let me leave the flat."

"You what? Are you, like, not under house arrest, but, you know, in protective custody or whatever?"

"Something like that. As they haven't got much else to go on, as I've clearly been singled-out, they want to make sure that nothing happens to me."

At just after nine, Kendrick called round with an update.

"Is there somewhere we can talk in private, Mr Barrowman?" He cast a sceptical eye over Liz.

"It's okay. This is my girlfriend. There's nothing you can't say in front of her."

He screwed up his face, as if he didn't approve of the idea, but proceeded to speak anyway. "Since you left the station, we've managed to contact most of the other people in your old counselling group, bar Jeffrey Fuller and Michelle Rouse. In all likelihood, they're working late or are out for the day, and hopefully, we'll track them down in the coming hours. Of those we've located, none have reported any unusual occurrences taking place over the last few days. Therefore, at this early stage, it would appear that you have, for reasons that are not altogether clear, been selected as a point of first contact."

"By Jeffrey Fuller, you mean? Have you looked into his background? Do you know what he's been up to all these years? Has he been in some kind of institute? Is that why I received that call regarding him at the office the other day?"

"We don't know yet, Mr Barrowman. But until we find them, both Mr Fuller and Miss Rouse, are suspects in the killing."

"Miss Rouse?" I couldn't stop myself from saying. "So Michelle never married, then?"

"Not as far as far as we're aware – looks like she lives alone."

"And what about Doctor Rabie? On the news they said that his body had been mutilated. What did they mean by that?"

"Sorry, Mr Barrowman. At present, I can't discuss details of the crime scene. The corpse was only discovered a handful of hours ago. Our forensics team is still sweeping the area for prints, hairs, fibres et cetera. We'll know more in the next twelve to twenty-four hours."

"And what about me now? Can I go out? Can I travel anywhere?"

"Best not to. Like I said, for whatever reason, whoever sent that photograph and mocked-up obituary wants you involved. With a link firmly established between you and Doctor Rabie, it would be logical to assume that the killer is someone known to you. Maybe it is Fuller, and maybe he's trying to make some kind of statement. Therefore, it would be unwise for you to be in any way exposed. For the time being, we ask you to remain here, at your home, at all times."

I clicked on the *Native American Folklore and Legends* link, opening a black and white homepage with the outline of an Indian chief in a feathered headdress as the background.

"Here." Liz leaned over me. "If you type, erm…I don't know: horned owl into that search engine thing, I bet it'll come up with a few pictures."

After a few moments, a new screen appeared with dozens of different depictions of the horned owl on it. I scrolled down until coming across what the site called *the horned owl, a portent of imminent death.*

"Told you. That shape you sketched out at work is pretty much identical."

"Yeah, you're right." It was uncanny, eerily so.

"Pity there's not much information on here, nothing 'bout the origins of the symbol, the story behind it, stuff like that." She paused for a moment. "And look, if you can't leave the flat, then why don't I get up dead early tomorrow, like six or something, jump on the train down to Portobello, go see my dad's old mate, show him a picture of that horned owl and see what he says? That way, we'll know a whole lot more about all of this than we do now."

Chapter Eleven

All morning I was mad on edge. I couldn't stop thinking about the past, Jeffrey Fuller, the things he'd said and done; the true state of his mind back then. In particular, I recalled one incredibly tetchy session where Rabie had encouraged him to speak frankly about the incident with his mother (although, the true extent of what had actually happened that day was always clouded in uncertainty, boastful embellishment then frantic denial). For some reason, Fuller got into a heated argument with Helen, who had perhaps tired of the same self-deceiving charade.

"But what if I crept into *your* bedroom with a knife–" he said, "when you were naked. What if I forced you to do things you didn't want to do? What then, eh?"

"I'd fight back, that's what. You're such a pathetic weakling, I'd take the knife from your hand and shove it up your arse."

Everyone laughed.

"Oh, you would, would you?" When angry, Jeffrey's whole body used to shake, like someone with Parkinson's disease. "I reckon there'd be a very different outcome. I reckon I'd slice you up good and proper, shutting your dirty mouth once and for all."

At this peak of nastiness, Rabie interceded.

"Jeffrey, please." He raised both hands, palms upturned. "Let's not turn the session into some kind of sadistic fantasy, the kinds of delusions which are probably at the root of all your problems."

"Delusions! If I'm subject to delusions, then what am I doing here?"

"You're here because you need to distinguish between what's real and what's not. You need to be able to function in your everyday life."

I can't remember what happened next, or if that was the end of that particular discussion. Only later, as we were all getting ready to leave, Fuller must've said something else to Rabie, something abusive or threatening, because the doctor asked him to stay behind to clear the air or talk things through to 'a logical conclusion' – a favourite stock phrase of his. But Fuller refused, saying, 'If anyone deserves a knife up their arse, it's you, you incompetent bastard'.

But had Fuller, over a decade later, really killed three people? Had he finally done something that would make everyone take him seriously?

The front door swinging open disturbed my thoughts.

"Bloody hell." Liz met me in the hallway again. "Those coppers are proper thorough." She stood on tiptoes and brushed her lips against my cheek. "Made me empty my bags and everything."

"Did you buy something?" I pointed to the carrier bag in her hand. "Did you find anything out?"

"Yeah, yeah, been an interesting morning. Come on. Let's go through to the kitchen. I'll show you, tell you all about it."

We went and sat at the kitchen table.

"Right. Billy, my dad's old mate, recognised the symbol straight away, got all excited, he did, telling me about its probable origins and what it may mean."

"Which is?"

"Well, he says the horned owl really is a symbol of death, that the Choctaw Indians, one of the five civilised tribes, who come from Mississippi and Alabama, used to call it Ishkitini, and that if you saw the horned owl, it meant that someone, usually a child was going to die. Reckons there's loads of folkloric stories regarding the owl, but he couldn't remember 'em all of the top of his head."

"So, we're on the right track with the markings cut into the two corpses at the hotel, and, presumably, Rabie, we're dealing with a maniac killer trying to assume the role of some ghostly prophet of doom."

Our eyes met. Neither of us spoke for a few moments.

"So what's in the bag?"

"Oh, that's just it." Liz slid a decorative, antique wooden box out of the carrier bag. On the lid was an intricately carved horned owl – or something very close to it. "A huge coincidence, but Bill had this piece on his stall, reckons it only came in the other day, said the box is hundreds of years old, that the carving is of Ishkitini. Reckons it's a proper desirable trinket in its own right, but he done me a pretty good deal on it."

I took the box and turned it around in my hands, pushing the top open to reveal a long, narrow silk-lined compartment.

"And did he say what it was used for?"

"To conceal a weapon: a dagger."

"A dagger?"

"Yeah. But like I said, he couldn't remember all the horned owl stories. So what we need to do next is get hold of a copy of this book he mentioned." She took a scrap of paper from her pocket. *"A Complete Guide to Native American Folklore*, was half-tempted to stop off in central London, go to one of those big shops on Oxford Street or Charing Cross Road, but thought it best to get back here as soon as I could."

"Don't worry. We might be able to—" two knocks sounded against the front door.

"Mr Barrowman?" Kendrick opened up and shouted down the hallway.

"In the kitchen." I slipped the box back inside the carrier bag.

"Ah, here you are.' He walked into the room. 'Hope I'm not interrupting anything, but we really need you to come down to the station again. There have been some slightly confusing developments, and you're the only man who could possibly shed light onto things."

"Developments? What kinds of developments?"

"All in good time, Mr Barrowman. I've got a car waiting outside."

"Right," said Watson, "as Detective Inspector Kendrick has no doubt made you aware, there have been some interesting developments overnight. Firstly, and quite worryingly, we still haven't been able to ascertain the whereabouts of either Mr Fuller or Miss Rouse."

"I see. That is worrying, considering everything that's happened."

"Indeed. Although, in the interim, we've looked into Mr Fuller's background, unearthing some important information."

"Was he in an Institute?"

"Yes. A secure housing unit on the Norfolk coast. By all accounts, he's had, as you predicted, a rather complicated life since the last time you saw each other – sectioned over a dozen times, arrested, been in and out of institutes and treatment programmes – but was never, ultimately, seen as a danger to the wider community, only to himself."

This sounded like the Jeffrey Fuller I'd known.

"Did the secure housing unit have any record of trying to contact me for information about Jeffrey?"

"No. Whoever called your office was not a member of staff – although the time lines do overlap."

"Time lines?"

"Yes. Around the time of the first murders Fuller went missing." Watson fixed his stern eyes on me, as if to confirm the significance of this. "That brings us on to Miss Rouse. Did you know that she kept a diary?" I shook my head. In all our time together she never mentioned one to me. "Well, she did. A very, erm...comprehensive diary. We found several dozen volumes when we searched her house." He handed me some photocopied sheets of paper. "We'll leave these selected samples with you for half an hour or so, then come back and ask you a few related questions. Once you read them, I'm sure you'll realise their importance."

I flicked through the pages, checking the dates neatly printed out at the top of each entry. In all, they had selected three samples, one from March 1985, around the time we were in the counselling sessions, one from June 1989, when

Michelle and I were living together, and a much more recent one, January 1993 – why, I was about to found out.

27th February 1985

It's nearly midnight. My parents are asleep in the next room. I can hear my father's light yet persistent snoring, which I find strangely soothing. I've just got back from the big séance that Helen and Riordan were talking about for weeks. What a letdown! I thought everyone was going to take it seriously. I thought we all agreed that there are things in this world that we don't fully understand, things that could be contributing to our conditions, to why we don't feel happy or content with life. But the others, including my clingy admirer, Nigel, were happy for the whole evening to descend into farce. As soon as we turned out the lights, lit the candles, and set up the Ouija board, they started giggling like little kids who've never been in a darkened room before, like we were a bunch of lusty, lecherous morons playing spin the bottle. All of which left me fuming. Every time Nigel tried to put his arm around me, I roughly pushed him away. It took a good hour before they realised the seriousness of the situation, the importance of what we were about to undertake, and how it could help us better understand ourselves. When Jeffrey's hand (and I really admired the way he took control of things) was directed across the table, spelling out: You will all die a horrible death, I knew there was, despite everyone's protests, saying Jeffrey was moving his hand of his own accord, more than a grain of truth in the prediction. From an early age, I've known that this will be the case – whether it's at my own hand or that of another, is the only thing that remains unclear.

On the way home Nigel got all possessive and weird again. I don't like it when he acts like that, pushing and shoving me around. He says it's the medication, but I know for a fact he doesn't take it half the time. And when I say I don't want to hang around with him anymore, he threatens to kill himself, to kill us both. He's such a drama queen. That's why I like spending so much time with Jeffrey. In front of the others he's a complete dick, but when we're alone he's the sweetest, most soulful and intelligent person I've ever met. If only I could let Nigel down gently, it would free up much more time to spend with Jeffrey. We'd be able to explore each other's minds. We'd be able to push things out further than we have ever done before.

I put the papers aside. Only vaguely did I remember the night of the so-called séance, but the events in my mind didn't match those in Michelle's diary. Yes, one of the girls had dug up an old Ouija board from somewhere. Yes, we did sit around in candlelight. But, to the best of my memory, Michelle was the most cynical person present, calling the whole thing superstitious nonsense. In fact, I'm sure she insisted that the two of us leave early. Because as soon as we arrived, Jeffrey raided the drinks cabinet, drank half a bottle of cognac neat, and was sick everywhere. As for my histrionics, the things Michelle complains about in the second and last paragraph, they may've had some truth to them. I was terribly dramatic back then, but I never pushed her around, I never laid a finger on her, or anyone else, for that matter – it just wasn't in my nature. And I certainly don't remember ever threatening suicide, not to a girl who'd cut her own wrists several times before. It was like reading things written by someone else, about a person I'd never met before. Moreover, the words as I heard them in my head didn't even sound like Michelle. Most troubling of all, though, I had no idea that she'd been seeing Jeffrey outside of the group, that she considered him to be anything other than a horrible, smarmy, twisted bastard. To think of them conducting some kind of secret friendship behind my back just didn't seem possible.

I picked up the next sheet of paper.

6th June 1989

Early hours, sitting at the kitchen table in pitch blackness, muggy, hot, can't sleep (again!!!) How I have I got myself into this position: living with someone I despise, someone I can't bear to be around? I feel trapped, manipulated, a prisoner. Whenever I'm close to Nigel, it's as if he's sucking the very life from me. The jealousy, the constant interrogations (yesterday, he insisted that I strip down to my underwear, so he could sniff me all over, so he could tell if I'd been with another man) are wearing me down. His behaviour is so erratic. From one minute to the next I don't know what he's going to do or say. If I ever try and show him any affection, if we ever sleep together, he's so rough and domineering, as if he's got to prove a point, to put me in my place, to show me that he's a real big man. There's no tenderness or intimacy – all the things I desperately need from life. Why can't he see that? Why can't he treat me as an equal not a possession? If I had anywhere else to go, bar my parents' house – which would only lead down the same dark road as before – I'd be out of the door, bags packed, in a shot, never to return. Even my counsellor is advising me to get away from Nigel, encouraging me to make a new start. But at least he's hanging onto that job at the council – the thought of having him around all day makes my skin crawl, makes me want to cut myself again. When will this nightmare end? When will I be free?

Again I stopped reading at the end of the entry and put the papers aside. Again I was completely perplexed by Michelle's words, as I'd always considered this particular period–'87 to '89–to have been the best of our relationship. We'd just moved in together, were deeply in love, held hands everywhere we went, couldn't get enough of each other. Five or six times a day, she rang the office just to tell me that she loved me, that she couldn't wait until I got home. In the evenings, she'd prepare a lovely meal, we'd drink a glass or two of wine, listen to music, take long, lazy baths together. In regards to our sex life, our lovemaking was always slow, soft and considered, full of the intimacy she claims was lacking (and I know it was, because I'd missed and longed for it ever since we split up). There were no jealous scenes. I never insisted that she strip so I could check for signs of infidelity. It was as if she'd written an alternative version of reality, where she'd completely reversed true life events. The only question was why?

I picked up the final sheet, the final entry, a shorter but no less disconcerting entry.

11th January 1993

Another letter from Nigel. Why won't he leave me alone? It's been over two years now. But every week, without fail, a letter lands on my doormat, full of the same threats and accusations. If I didn't have Jeffrey to confide in, to lean on, I don't know what I'd do. He's so intelligent and level-headed. He tells me to make notes, to keep track of everything, that even if I don't want to open the letters, I should file them away in chronological order. That way, when the police get involved, I'll have a clear record of what undoubtedly constitutes serious harassment. Only I'm scared. If Nigel, after all this time, still can't let things go, if he can't get on with his life, then I'm certain he'll come looking for me, I'm certain he'll make good on one of his outrageous threats, that my horrible death will be at his hands.

Chapter Twelve

I told the police that the diaries were complete nonsense, that I had no idea why Michelle had dreamed up such outrageous falsehoods, that our relationship, right up to the very end, had been a relatively happy one.

"Ten years," said Watson, "that's how long Miss Rouse kept this, complete nonsense as you call it, up for. Highly unlikely, don't you agree?"

"Yes, of course. But what you've got to understand is that we were both suffering from mental health problems. We didn't think or act like normal people. Michelle had attempted suicide numerous times. She could be a very manipulative, highly-strung young woman – one moment up, the next moment down. Completely benign comments could send her into a dark depression. Perhaps the diaries were just a coping mechanism, perhaps she did feel suffocated by me at times, and this was her way of expressing herself."

Watson and Kendrick exchanged a brief, doubtful glance.

"Look. What's actually happening here? Have I become the number one murder suspect simply because my old girlfriend wrote some harsh words about me?"

"No, no, not at all," said Watson. "But put yourself in our position – three grisly murders, you're the only concrete link, on searching your former girlfriend's house we find boxes of old diaries painting you in a far from flattering light. We have to follow-up on this information, Mr Barrowman. You understand that, don't you?"

Reluctantly, I nodded my head.

"And in light of the diaries, we took another look at your medical records." Watson held up a file. "It says here that you had serious problems with the anti-psychotic medication you were prescribed, that you often became argumentative, unreasonable, that you struggled to distinguish between what was real and what was not, that you suffered from blackouts, and couldn't remember what you'd said or done. There's even mention of you assaulting a nurse."

"All true. But that was a long, long time ago. I was just a boy – seventeen or eighteen years old. The incidents you just mentioned were, erm…isolated, confined to a particular three-month period when I trialled a hugely controversial drug, one that was later deemed unsuitable for my condition, and quickly removed from the market."

"Okay, okay, Mr Barrowman, that's enough for today. Once again, thank you for your time. I know how stressful this must be, but, like I said before, you're the only link we have between the murders." He got to his feet. "Why don't you go home now and get some rest?"

When I got back to the flat, I found a note and another carrier bag on the kitchen table.

Nigel,
Thought since you weren't going to be about, that I'd pop back into London and get that book. Didn't have a chance to look at it myself – I'm at The Samaritans again tonight, so won't be able to see you until sometime tomorrow. Try not to worry about things too much. We can have a good chat then.
Hope everything went all right at the police station
Thinking of you
Liz
XXX

A Complete Guide to Native American Folklore had a glossy cover depicting an Indian chief, complete with feathered headdress. The foreword, penned by a renowned scholar, eulogised the Native American way of life, the purity of their philosophy and worldview, their unique spiritual attachment to the land, the antithesis of modern environmental excesses that had ravaged the planet.

I turned to the contents page and ran a finger down the list of sections and subsections, eventually finding a chapter entitled *Ishkitini: The Legend of the Horned Owl*.

Ishkitini: The Legend of the Horned Owl

Wapasha was born to one of the Choctaw tribes most respected families. A strong healthy boy, he grew into a fine, muscular, handsome young man, a prolific hunter, skilful rider, and brave, valorous, if hot-headed and sometimes impetuous warrior. From an early age, Wapasha had been betrothed to Isi, who would become one of the tribe's most dazzling beauties, a squaw with shiny coal-black hair, dark skin, strong white teeth and a full, supple figure. As young children, Wapasha and Isi had been almost inseparable. Each day they played together, held hands, would often be found in a shaded grove, whispering into each other's ears, laughing and joking around. To impress Isi, a teenage Wapasha would perform daring feats, like walking on his hands, throwing machetes into tree trunks or lassoing wild horses. As they approached adulthood, becoming man and wife was inevitable, truly a match made in the heavens above.

When Isi fell pregnant with their first child, there was much rejoicing in the settlement. For these young people were the perfect embodiments of the Choctaw way of living. In such uncertain times, with white frontiersmen forcibly removing Native Americans from their sacred lands, waging bloody battles, wiping entire tribes from the face of the earth, young and old were looking forward to welcoming a new generation of Choctaw Indian into the world.

However, when Isi went into labour, a true misfortune befell the parents-to-be: a horned owl was sighted in a nearby tree, a terrible omen, one that usually heralded the death of an infant. No sooner was the baby safely delivered than the owl let out a fearsome screech, one that was heard for miles around.

When Wapasha presented his newborn son to Chief Antiman, therefore, the wise old man gravely shook his head.

"What is it?" asked Wapasha. "I bring you my firstborn child, a new descendent of the great Choctaw line."

The Chief pointed to the tree from which the horned owl had just alighted.

"Ishkitini," he said, a solemn expression etched across his wrinkled, weather-beaten face. "At the moment your son was born, the horned owl screeched. Wapasha, you know what this means. Wherever Ishkitini ventures, death quickly follows. Within seven days, your son will be dead."

This news sent Wapasha and Isi into a deep, disbelieving depression, for their healthy newborn child could not have been a more perfect representation of their love for each other.

"Why?" Wapasha ground a balled fist into the palm of his other hand. "Why have the Gods cursed us like this? What have we done to deserve such a cruel injustice?"

Beside himself, Wapasha rushed to see Chief Antiman again.

"I've been expecting you." The Chief gestured for Wapasha to sit opposite him. "I feel your pain, but you must remember, life is not separate from death, it just looks that way. And what is life? – the flash of a firefly in the night, the breath of a buffalo in the wintertime, the little shadow which runs across the grass and loses itself in the sunset?"

"You talk in riddles," said Wapasha. "There's so little time. Can anything be done to reverse the prophecy of the horned owl, this horrible curse which has befallen my family?"

"No," said the elder. "The shadow of death cannot be removed from your newborn son. You must accept it and move on."

"But I—"

"Listen," Chief Antiman interrupted, "or your tongue will make you deaf. We do not inherit this Earth from our ancestors, we borrow it from our children. And in your case,

there will be more children. You and Isi are young and strong. Enjoy the time you have left with your child. Rejoice. Always remember him in your hearts and minds. Don't let yesterday use up too much of today. Try and—"

"But why?" cried Wapasha, shooting to his feet.

"Wapasha, calm yourself. This anger will consume you forever more if you do not rein it in. Remember the story of the wise old man who tried to teach his grandson of such things. "A fight is going on inside of me", he said to the boy. "It is a terrible fight and it is between two wolves. One is evil – he is anger, envy, sorrow, regret, greed, arrogance, self-pity, guilt, resentment, inferiority, lies, false pride, superiority, self-doubt and ego. The other is good – he is joy, peace, love, hope, serenity, humility, kindness, benevolence, sincerity, empathy, generosity, truth, compassion and faith. This same fight is going on inside of you and inside of every other person, too". The grandson thought about this for a moment and then he asked his grandfather, "Which wolf will win?" The old man replied, "The one you feed".

That night, Wapasha suffered a terrible nightmare. In this vivid, disturbing dream, a horned owl swooped down from the skies, snatching his child from Isi's arms, whisking him off high up into the sky. And no matter how hard Wapasha gave chase, he was powerless to stop the bird from disappearing out of sight.

Wapasha woke up screaming.

"What is it?" said Isi, comforting her husband.

"No–Nothing, a bad dream." He sat up and rubbed his hands up and down his face. "Isi, I cannot accept this terrible curse. Within the hour, I will leave the settlement with our son. Under cover of darkness, I will take him to a place where nothing or no-one can harm him."

At that moment, they heard the screech of the horned owl, the one the elder had warned them about. Both raced over to the crib, finding their newborn son, open-eyed, wiggling his arms and legs, with what looked like a smile breaking out across his soft fleshy face.

"I must leave now," proclaimed Wapasha. "Wrap the baby up tightly. When the seven days are up, I will return to the settlement with our son. On that you have my word."

Once outside, Wapasha gathered the baby up in a bundle, clambered upon a horse, and rode through the blackness of the early morn. Within minutes he could hear the hooting of the horned owl, giving chase. For many miles, Wapasha rode furiously, not once letting up. But every time he glanced over his shoulder, he could see the winged pursuer out of the corner of his eye, getting closer and closer.

It was then Wapasha knew that he would have to face the horned owl himself; that he would have to try and kill the demon bird once and for all. Directing his horse over to the bow of a fallen tree, he carefully stowed his son away in the hollowed-out trunk, in such a manner, it would be almost impossible for the horned owl to get at him. Unsheathing his machete, Wapasha swung round just as the owl appeared, landing on the dusty ground, not six feet away.

"Come," said Wapasha, raising his weapon. "If you want my son, you must get past me first."

To his shock, the horned owl started talking to him in a clear, human voice, "You are a brave, worthy young man, a man of spirit and conviction. But why waste your energy? You know that once the horned owl appears, a prophecy has already been foretold."

"I do not care," said Wapasha, lunging forward, swinging the blade with terrible force, intent on killing the bird with one true blow – but all he sliced through was thin air.

"Over here."

Wapasha swung round, to where the horned owl had reappeared.

"It is better to have less thunder in the mouth, Wapasha, more lightning in the hand. Your efforts are useless. I give you one last opportunity to say goodbye to your son. Then I will take him from this world."

Enraged, Wapasha lunged at the horned owl once again. And once again, his flailing blade sliced through nothing more than air. Only this time, when he swung back round, all he heard was flapping wings, and when he looked up to the sky, all he could see was the horned owl disappearing across the horizon, carrying the bundle containing his baby son.

Unsure of the story's significance, I opened an internet session and typed: ishkitini, horned owl, Native American folklore, Choctaw owl myth and the like, into a search engine, widening the scope of the original search I did with Liz last night. After scrolling down the list of results, I found a link to an article by Doctor Rabie, an extract from his one and only published book, *Is There Any Such Thing As a Feeling?*

The Boy Who Could Not Escape His Own Fate

In Choctaw folklore, there is a famous story about a horned owl that prowled the night killing men and animals. A hugely superstitious people, the Choctaw believed that when Ishkitini screeched, it meant sudden death, much like a murder. In one variation of the story, a brave young warrior refuses to accept that his newborn son has been cursed to die, when the owl is heard soon after his birth. Whisking the child away, he attempts to reverse fate, to fight back, physically, at the cost of his own life. But Ishkitini follows after him, takes the child and fulfils the prophecy.

In many deluded patients suffering from schizophrenic episodes, I have witnessed a similar phenomenon. Through suicide attempt, self-harm or self-intoxication, they have attempted to escape a version of their own fate, a version that has built up in their heads, waging a battle like the young Choctaw warrior. One particular patient, a very troubled young man who participated in experimental group sessions, heard voices, voices which urged him to take his own mother by force – sexually. For many months, if not years, the patient battled these voices in his head, only to succumb one morning, sensing that fulfilment of the rape fantasy was inevitable. However, he was unable to see it through to the end. And herein lies the conundrum: does a patient have to obey the voice in their head, playing things out to a concrete conclusion, before they will be able to move on in life? Put simply: if they feel that they have to cut their own wrists, will the impulse only be neutralised once they actually, physically slice their skin with a blade?

Undoubtedly, the patient Rabie wrote about all those years ago was Jeffrey Fuller – anybody who had attended our sessions would have recognised the description. Had Jeffrey, therefore, read Doctor's Rabie's book, and resented it so much, seeing it as far too revealing, that he was determined to have his revenge?

Chapter Thirteen

The following afternoon, Kendrick called round again.

"Ah, Mr Barrowman." He placed a thick file on the kitchen table. "Apologies for disturbing you on a Sunday, but Senior Detective Inspector Watson wanted me to have another chat with you, to clear a few things up re: the alleged correspondence with Miss Rouse."

"Oh, right. I see."

"First things first: we've completed the check on the computers at your place of work, and found nothing out of the ordinary. If the photograph you received in the post last Monday was indeed a piece of skilful photo-shopping – which we're pretty certain it wasn't – it wasn't done in any of the council offices."

"Okay. That's good, I suppose."

Kendrick took some papers from the file. "Now I'd like to show you a few sample letters taken from Miss Rouse's residence."

"The letters I'd supposedly been sending her for the last five years?"

"That's right." He handed me the bundle. "As you can see, they are rather, erm…to the point."

I took the photocopies and looked them over. Each one was short, typed, having more in common with a poison pen letter than any substantial form of correspondence. One read: *Come back to me or I'll kill you*. Another: *I'm going to make you pay for this*. Another still: *Look, Michelle. The more you ignore me, the closer I get. Don't you understand? If you don't move back in with me, I'll punish you and all those you hold dear.*

I looked up from the letters.

"Like I said, Detective Inspector, after me and Michelle

66

split up, I never, ever tried to contact her again. You have my word on that. It was too painful."

"But like *we* said yesterday, it seems beyond the realm of reasonable possibility for someone to keep up a false diary and a false series of letters for this length of time. Are you sure that you didn't write them? Maybe in your darker moments, maybe when you forgot to take your medication you—"

"But I haven't been on proper medication for years! I don't think I should ever have been prescribed half the things I was prescribed in the first place. If I were to hazard a guess, and remember, I know Michelle as well, if not better, than anyone else, I'd say she's kept up this fictitious correspondence to make people feel sorry for her, to play the victim. I bet the whole thing has got little or nothing to do with me, more her and her various hang-ups and neuroses."

"And what about her relations with Jeffrey Fuller?"

"Maybe they're a fantasy, too."

Kendrick's face momentarily betrayed something, something hard to interpret.

"What is it?"

"Well, when questioned, the other members of your old counselling group corroborated that to a certain extent. Not one of them could believe that Mr Fuller and Miss Rouse were ever in a relationship, that they were anything other than enemies. Many went so far as to suggest that Miss Rouse despised Mr Fuller and everything about him."

Despite feeling vindicated, I didn't gloat or say I told you so. The situation, from my point of view, with regards the diary and the letters, still felt precarious.

"Where does that leave us, then? I saw the news earlier, that you're now actively searching for Jeffrey and Michelle."

"That's right. So sudden and unexpected were their disappearances, with no word to friends or loved ones, places of work or staff at the institute, we're extremely concerned for their well-being."

"What? You don't think Jeffrey's taken Michelle against her will, do you? That he's trying to exact some kind of twisted revenge for everything that happened in those counselling sessions all those years ago?"

"It's a possibility, Mr Barrowman."

We talked for another quarter of an hour before Kendrick got up to leave.

"And what about me?" I asked. "Can I leave the flat now? Can I go to work tomorrow as normal?"

"Ideally we'd like you remain here for the time being. Realistically speaking, though, it's hugely unlikely that someone who'd just committed three brutal murders would risk trying to get at you in some way. Therefore, we're happy for you to go about your day to day activities, work included. To be safe, we'll have an officer follow you around, have a car parked outside your office, and here overnight."

"Hi, Nigel," said Liz. "Thought I'd give you a quick call. How's things? What's the latest?"

I told her all about the diary entries and the letters, how Michelle claimed a five-year correspondence, a reign of terror and harassment, when I'd never written her a single line.

"And they're all conveniently type-written so the police can't identify your handwriting? Bit fishy, that. And not to be rude, but your ex sounds like a proper psycho bitch."

As an assessment, it was pretty accurate. But I was more pleased by the nature of Liz's unconditional support, that she believed everything I'd just told her.

"Talking of exes, I made a few phone calls this afternoon. I spoke to Mick and few of my dad's old mates, proper hard men."

"About Scott, you mean?"

"Yeah. They went down the boozer straight away – mob-handed. Apparently he always has a Sunday lunch-time drink in the Barking Dog, by the station."

"What happened? Did he confess to attacking me? Did

they attack him?"

"That's just the thing, Nigel. He swears he never laid a finger on you, that it wasn't him who gave you that beating the other night."

"What? But if it wasn't him, then who was it?"

Chapter Fourteen

On my desk, amongst a mountain of unopened correspondence, outstanding claim forms, risk and assessment surveys and pothole statistics, was a memo from the Deputy-Director, stapled to a copy of a letter from a Mrs Forbes-Powers, with several sentences highlighted in fluorescent marker:

...Mr Barrowman's obtuse manner...rude and unhelpful...the temerity to slam the phone down on me – a taxpayer!!!

I read the letter from the beginning, soon realising it was from the woman who'd called late last week regarding dog mess on the pavement. I turned back to the memo.

In my capacity as Deputy-Director, I shouldn't have to deal with such middling complaints. Mrs Forbes-Powers is a respected member of the local community, a lady with local government connections. V. disappointed. Have contacted personnel re: making your attendance on a customer care training course an utmost priority.

"Nige!" Michael walked in through the open door. "You're back! Christ! Let's hope the police catch this maniac soon then we won't risk losing you again. I don't know how I got by without you." He glanced at my desk. "And sorry about all that paperwork. I had to go to a few important meetings, so the office was literally unmanned. Sure it won't take too long to file that lot away, though." He gave me a blokey, down the pub slap on the back. "Oh, and can you do me a big, big favour – dig out the Howard File, the old boy who tripped over that uneven paving slab and broke both his wrists."

"The Howard File? I thought you'd signed it off and sent it up to Legal months ago."

"Yeah, me too." Michael pulled a suitably bemused expression. "Must've slipped through the net, now I'm getting it in the neck from Mackintosh, who reckons we could be on very dodgy ground due to the delay."

My phone started to ring.

"Hello, Risk and Assessment."

"Hi, Nige, just Gemma from reception here. There's a gentleman in the foyer who wants to speak to you."

I glanced out of the window – police car, policeman still in place.

"Oh, right. Did he give a name and tell you what it was regarding?"

"Erm, no" – a ditzy giggle – "to be honest, I didn't ask. But you'll come through, yeah?"

In the foyer area, I found a well-dressed, sandy-haired man of middle age sitting on one of the seventies-style faux leather seats

"Mr Barrowman?" He got to his feet and offered me his hand. "I'm Graham Bannister. Nice to meet you."

"What can I do for you, Mr Bannister?"

"Well, at this stage, I'm not entirely sure. As you're aware, Michelle Rouse went missing from her home several days ago. In that time, no one, including her family and close friends, has heard from her. Yesterday, her parents engaged my services in hope of—"

"Your services?"

"That's correct. I'm what you would call a private investigator. And I'm sorry to have come to your workplace unannounced, but as it's around lunch-time now, I was hoping that you might spare me half an hour or so of your time, to answer a few important questions regarding Miss Rouse's potential whereabouts."

I darted yet another look out of the window. Again:

police car, policeman in situ.

"It's okay," said Bannister, as if reading my mind. "I had a quick chat with P.C. Gilmore outside, and explained the situation. He's cleared it with his senior officer."

"Really?"

"Yes. I'm former S.A.S., you see, and have a few contacts at police H.Q., old friends. So why don't I drive to that pub just down the road, buy us a drink, and then we can have a chat?"

"As I'm sure you appreciate" – Bannister placed two pints of bitter on our table – "Miss Rouse's parents are sick with worry. After all, this is their only child we're talking about. And with all the problems they've faced over the years – the depression, self-harming, suicide attempts – for Miss Rouse to disappear so unexpectedly, just when she seemed to have attained a perfect balance in her life, work and relationships, is a particularly cruel blow."

"How do you mean – the perfect balance? Has she got a good job now? Is she seeing someone special?"

Bannister looked at me questioningly. "Are you saying that you don't know?"

"Yes. Because I don't! Despite what the diaries and letters found at Michelle's home indicate, I've never once phoned, written or tried to contact her in the five years since we parted."

Bannister screwed up his face, as if my outburst had just confirmed the impression he'd already formed of me: pathological liar, weirdo, nutcase, someone not to be trusted.

"Well, on that I'll have to reserve judgment, because, as you know, pretty compelling evidence has come to light suggesting otherwise. But, in answer to your question, Miss Rouse recently obtained a T.E.F.E.L. qualification, enabling her to teach abroad. Having worked in a local junior school for a few years, gaining essential experience, she was about to embark upon a career, a vocation, if you will, as her parents were convinced that she was a born teacher."

This was yet another piece of information that I found hard to believe, because it was so contradictory. Granted, Michelle was highly intelligent, perceptive, articulate, even, but she had no patience whatsoever, a short temper, a complete lack of interpersonal skills, qualities essential for any teacher.

"In addition to her professional plans, Miss Rouse had just started a serious relationship."

"Really? With who?"

"That her parents don't know. After her relationship with you failed so spectacularly, Miss Rouse was very secretive about her private life. She wanted, so she told her mother and father, to make sure that she'd met the right person before making the whole thing official."

"Do you think it could be Jeffrey Fuller?"

"That's certainly a possibility. And that's where I'm heading later this afternoon – to the secure housing unit on the Norfolk coast. But, and I see no reason in concealing the fact, Miss Rouse's parents have requested that I focus my attention upon you, finding out where you were and what you were doing around the time of their daughter's disappearance."

"Me? Why?"

"Put yourself in their position: the diaries, the letters – all bearing an Ilford postmark – the fact you've been questioned by the police in regards to the killings. Wouldn't you, if you were them, see Nigel Barrowman as prime suspect in your daughter's disappearance?"

"Erm, yes I suppose I would. But I assure you, I have nothing to do with any of this."

As if still reserving judgment, Bannister asked a series of questions related to the photograph and obituary, information I was sure he was already in possession of. Then he said something very odd:

"Did you ever cheat on Miss Rouse during your relationship? Were you ever interested in, how can one put it: deviant sexual practises, S&M, role play, rape fantasies, maybe even intercourse with another man?"

"No! We were very much in love. Our relations were normal. I would never have dreamed of cheating on Michelle or of becoming involved in any of the sick things you just mentioned."

"Okay, okay, Mr Barrowman, we'll leave it there for now. Thank you for being so frank and upfront with me. You'd have been well within your rights to tell me where to go, to refuse to talk, to cooperate in any way."

"That's because I've got nothing to hide."

Just as I was about to leave off for the day, the telephone started to ring.

"Risk and Assessment, how can I help?"

"Is that Barrowman?" barked a very well-spoken man.

"That's right."

"Terrence Biles here, Deputy-Director."

"Oh, hello, Sir, how can I help?"

"You don't know? You haven't seen the memo I sent last week?"

"No, I mean, yes. What I mean is, I've been out of the office and—"

"I can't believe this! You receive a communiqué from senior management and you don't see fit to respond."

"I didn't realise that you wanted a response. I thought the matter was, erm…closed, that you'd recommended that I attend a training course."

"Of course the matter isn't closed, you imbecile. Moreover, your caviler *I couldn't care less* attitude is indicative of a much deeper malaise running throughout the junior ranks of local government. If a member of the public contacts your department, you should endeavour to provide exemplary customer service, even if it means going above and beyond the call of duty, even if it means contacting other departments yourself. To put the phone down on anyone is completely unacceptable."

I wanted to say: Shut up, you sanctimonious old prick. Over the last week, I've been caught up in three brutal killings, assaulted outside my own home, implicated in the disappearance of an old girlfriend, things far more important than some posh old woman moaning about dog shit on a pavement – but, of course, I remained silent.

"However," a slight softening of tone, "you have, due to the lady in question's almost saint-like magnanimity, been offered a chance to reprieve yourself."

"I have?"

"Yes. As luck would have it, Mrs Forbes-Powers lives a stone's throw away from your office. Have you got a pen to hand? Jot this down." He relayed the address, a street I knew well; just around the corner from my flat. "All this kindly, venerable woman would like you to do is call round, this very afternoon, as soon as you put the phone down, to have a look at the problem of dogs fouling the footpaths near her home. Requisition a camera, take photographs, act courteously and professionally, show her that you are taking her complaint seriously, mention the new dog bin and poop-scoop initiatives local authorities are hoping to put in place to encourage dog owners to clear up after their animals. Talk to the lady as if she's a human being, not some mental deficient put on earth merely to irritate you. Understood?"

Chapter Fifteen

"You've gotta do what?" P.C. Gilmore leaned on the steering-wheel, looking right and left, looking to take advantage of a gap in the ever thickening traffic. "Take photographs of dogshit?"

"Well, basically, yeah."

"Ha! And I thought I got all the crappy jobs 'round here. But if that's the case, I'll drop you off and pick you up in say, half-hour or so. Gotta get to the mall before it closes, see. It's me missus' birthday today, and I've left it a bit late to bag her up something special."

"No, no, don't worry. You don't have to do that. It's just around the corner. Let me get out wherever's easy. I can always make my own way back to the flat. It's literally five minutes away."

"Oh, I don't know 'bout that. If anything went wrong, the guv would hit the roof, 'specially after that pasting you took the other night."

"What could go wrong? I'll take a few quick photographs, offer a sincere apology on behalf of all the inconsiderate dog owners in the area, and probably be back at my place before you are."

He hesitated. "Erm, are you sure? I mean, you don't mind? It don't freak you out or nothing, being out on your own?"

"Not at all. I can get out here, and be where I need to be in no time." I pulled the door open a fraction, emitting a cold breeze, the hum of passing cars and the rumble of many idling engines.

"Okay. Cheers. I'll see you in 'bout half-hour, then."

"Mr Barrowman?" shouted a haughty, superior, very

familiar voice.

I lifted my head. Across the street, standing outside a towering three-storey house, was, presumably, Mrs Forbes-Powers, the hall light spilling from the front door illuminating her tall, slender shape.

I crossed over.

"Good afternoon. Mrs Forbes-Powers, I take it."

"That's correct, young man." She opened the garden gate and stepped out onto the pavement. "Thank you for taking the time to come out and see me."

"No problem."

"No problem!" she spluttered. "Well, that wasn't quite the case when I contacted your office last week, was it? Or when I wrote those two letters marked specifically for your attention?"

"Letters?"

"Oh, don't play dumb, pretending you haven't seen them. I suppose you passed each one on to the correct department, like the metaphorical buck – unread. That's the problem with you low-ranking civil servants: you've got no spunk, no drive or ambition. You think you can exist in your drab, grey little world, pottering around your drab, grey little office for forty-odd years and then retire on a nice comfortable pension. But life, I'm afraid, Mr Barrowman, isn't like that."

I didn't know what to say. Rich, well-educated people, the arrogance and assurance of the moneyed classes, had always unnerved me.

"And as you can see" – she gestured right and left – "the pavements are absolutely littered with dog mess, one lump after the other. It's almost impossible to avoid. It's like living on a farm or in some third world shanty town."

I looked in the direction her flailing arms were indicating, but it was too dark to make anything out.

"And while I appreciate that you are not personally responsible for this debacle, I'm sure you'll agree that something has to be done. If not, an elderly resident will slip and break their neck."

I told her that I fully understood, that the council had raised funds to install bins for the specific deposit of dog mess–dog bins–and that a poster campaign encouraging dog owners to buy a poop-scoop to clean after their animals was at the design stage.

"Poop-scoop? I can't see that catching on. People around here have no consideration. And besides, weren't you supposed to take some photographs?" She pointed to the camera bag hanging from my shoulder.

"Erm, yes I was, but I think it may well be too dark to—"

"Never mind, never mind." She turned on her heels. "I've got some in the house. Pictures you can present to your superiors first thing tomorrow morning, showing exactly how bad things have got. Follow me."

I followed her up the garden path and into the house, into a high-ceilinged hallway.

"Close the front door, will you?" she shouted from the depths of the house, having quickly disappeared.

I pushed the door to and waited, listening out for any sounds, but there were none. I shuffled forward, closer to the foot of the staircase, angling my head down the hallway, seeing that the door leading down to what was presumably a basement was open – which struck me as odd, but not in any significant way, not yet.

Heels clicked against the flooring; Mrs Forbes-Powers walked back down the hallway.

"Here." She handed me a set of Polaroid photographs, each picture featuring a close-up shot of a dog turd, some thick and coiled, others small and insignificant, or no more than splotches of runny brown matter spattered against a pavement. But none had any real context, in the sense of a landmark or road name in the background, so it was impossible to identify the location.

"Well? Pretty compelling evidence, eh?"

"Erm, yes. Only it's hard to tell exactly where these pictures have been taken. They're all incredibly close to the offending—"

"What are you talking about? Here." She snatched the

photographs from my hand, and gestured for me to step forward, closer to the light. "What about this one?"

I leaned forward to get a better look at the photograph – but it was the same as the others.

"Like I said: it would've been better if you'd have taken a step back, and included a point of local reference. That way, we'd have known exactly where the picture had been taken."

"Outrageous!" she cried. "I won't stand for it. Always making bloody excuses, you lot."

"It's no problem. I can easily call back tomorrow, first thing in the morning, and take some pictures then, to present to the Deputy-Director."

"The only thing you'll be doing tomorrow, you pathetic little grub, is nursing a sore head."

"What?"

Completely unexpectedly, with both hands, and with far more force than she seemed to possess, Mrs Forbes-Powers pushed me in the chest, pushed me backwards, through the open door, sending me tumbling down a set of concrete steps.

Chapter Sixteen

"There you go, old chap," I heard a well-spoken young man say, as he very carefully eased me up into a sitting position. "You certainly took one hell of tumble there, what? But, bar the odd cut and bruise, I don't think you've done any serious damage."

"Where – Where I am?" I said, rubbing my eyes.

"Well, to put it bluntly: you're in a bit of a pickle."

"What?"

"Look. Let's get you sat in a chair before we discuss your current predicament. Okay? Sound like a plan?"

Once seated, it still took a while before my eyes could focus properly, to take everything in, to assimilate my new surroundings: a sprawling basement, converted into a domestic living space. Open-plan, it was split into different sections, different rooms, the point of delineation marked by a change in furniture. The front room: a three-piece suit, an elegant walnut coffee table, a thick, expensive-looking oriental rug, a stuffed crocodile on top of it. To the right, a small dining table and two chairs, a shaded standing lamp which provided the only light. In the far corner, two single beds, one made-up, if the sheets were slightly crumpled, the other, stripped, with blankets piled neatly upon the mattress. Parallel was a white-tiled wet room, with shower, sink and toilet. To the left, a table tennis table, only half unfolded, as if a solo player had been getting in some practise, knocking a ball up against the inverted section. Hanging directly above the table was a piece of artwork that looked eerily familiar. Again I rubbed my eyes, in an attempt to refocus, not quite believing what I was looking at: a horned owl, the exact same symbol I'd seen in the photograph taken at the first murder scene.

"What's that on the wall?" I pointed.

"Oh, just an old African tribal symbol – not sure what it means. Although Mater, who spent the first twenty-odd years of her life out in Rhodesia, did tell me once. Maybe something to do with death or revenge, not completely sure. Here." He handed me a glass of water. "Drink this."

As I gulped back the water I was, for the first time, able to look my companion over. Tall, wiry, with lively blue eyes, a very neat side-parting to his shiny auburn hair, clean-shaven if slightly rosy cheeks, he wore a silk cravat, tucked into a very smart button-down shirt, which was, in turn, tucked into a pair of pressed, well-cut, almost hipster-style trousers, and shiny slip-on leather shoes with tassels.

"Better?" He took the empty glass from my hand.

"Yes. Thank you." I wiped my sleeve across my chin. "So, what is this place? Some sort of study, a writer's underground hideaway or artist's studio?"

"No." A wry, even anxious smile broke out across his face. "It's a prison."

"Prison? What do you mean?"

"Just that, I'm afraid, old boy. Mater up there has completely lost the plot. Keeps me hidden away here, under lock and key. I knew I shouldn't have dropped out of Cambridge like that, but I didn't think it was going to upset her this much."

"You're joking, right?"

"I wish I was," he said. "When I announced my plans – and to be completely truthful, I had made an awful mess of things, running up huge debts – Mater went berserk, couldn't face the embarrassment of telling her friends that I was a failure. Only child, see, bit of a prodigy, bit of a bookworm, bit of a wordsmith. Had high hopes for me did Mater, especially when she railroaded me into reading law. That's where the money's at, she said. With our family connections, you'll be a High Court judge one day. Or words to that effect."

"So what happened?"

"Pretty much what just happened to you, old boy. She

insisted I visit for a chat about the future, ushered me into the hall, and pushed me down the cellar steps."

"When? How long ago?"

"Can't say for certain, but it must be getting on for two, maybe three years now."

"Three years!" I couldn't believe what I was hearing. "But – But the police know I'm here. They'll come and rescues me – rescue us!"

"Been and gone, my good man, been and gone. Thought they had Mater for a moment, caught her on the hop. Yes. She certainly wasn't expecting the boys in blue to be hammering on the door all of forty minutes after pushing you down those steps. But she soon regained her composure, played her meek old widow bit to a tee, told them you'd stopped by, but would return tomorrow because it was too dark to take any photographs."

This was all too much to take in.

"I'm Gideon, by the way." He offered me his hand. "And you're Nigel, I believe. Glad to make your acquaintance. Now, if you're up to it, I can show you around the place… That's the boudoir, as it were." He pointed to the beds I'd already seen. "Bathroom, games rooms. And, most important of all, over there is the dumb waiter, access straight up to the kitchen. In about, erm" – he checked his wristwatch – "five minutes, Mater should send down an aperitif, a bloody strong vodka martini, if we're lucky. Approximately half an hour after that, dinner is served."

"Oh, so she at least provides you with some kind of sustenance, then?"

"More than just sustenance, Nigel." Gideon rubbed his hands together. "The woman is an amazing chef, prides herself on keeping a good table. To be perfectly honest with you, the meals are the only things that have kept me relatively sane."

"But why would she do this to you, her only son? Surely it can't just be because you dropped out of university."

"Well, maybe it was a straw to a camel's back type of scenario. Watching Pater die of pancreatic cancer wasn't easy for her. After that, I think she invested all her hopes in me – which was, unfortunately, too great a burden of expectation to bear. Not got much backbone, you see, not much mortar between the bricks, been seeing therapists since I was a teenager."

"I understand. Being an only child can be a struggle. But haven't you ever tried to escape?"

"Of course I have. But not for a while now. The place is pretty much impenetrable, soundproofed. I think the former owner used it as some kind of recording studio. We can hear, albeit faintly, what's going on upstairs, but no one can hear us down here. Put simply: we're trapped, helpless. Unless Mater comes to her senses, there really is no way out."

The dumb waiter rattled then dinged.

"Ah, excellent, drinks." Gideon rushed over and opened the hatch. "Oh yes!" He swung round with a large cocktail shaker and two long-stemmed glasses on a silver tray. "Looks like she's pulled out all the stops tonight. I bet there's enough in here for two stiff drinks apiece. Come on. Let's sit at the table."

Very carefully, Gideon poured out the drinks, handing me one of the elegant glasses.

"Chin-chin, Nigel, your good health."

"Yes, cheers." I took a sip of martini, so strong I couldn't help but cough. "Phew! That's, erm…certainly got a kick to it."

"Delicious, right on the money. Yes. A couple of these will make you talk about your relations all right."

I put my glass on the table. "Look, Gideon, I really need to get out of here. My life at the moment is extremely complicated. Your mother doesn't know what she's done, who she's really kidnapped. Lives could literally be at risk if I don't escape."

"I understand, old chap, but I don't want to sit here and fill you with false hope."

"But I'm helping the police investigate a triple murder. The main suspect is an old acquaintance of mine, so to the victims. My girlfriend is involved now. I—"

"Triple murder, hey? How exciting? What exactly have you got yourself mixed up in, then, old chap?"

As if the enormity of what had happened this evening had only just sunk in, I told him the whole story, in much the same way I'd told the police, omitting not a single detail.

"And this Jeffrey what-his-name has not been seen since the first murder? Hmm…well, not to sound flippant, but aren't you in the safest place, then? I mean, clearly he'll come after you, sooner rather than later, and would have to have supernatural powers to find you down here, what?"

"That's not the point. I need to find out what that owl symbol really means. I need to find out what has happened to Jeffrey and Michelle. More than anything, I need to make sure Liz is all right, that she hasn't got caught up in all of this."

"Understood," said Gideon. "Only I'm not sure how sympathetic Mater is going to be."

Chapter Seventeen

"Pass the vino, will you?" Gideon placed a knife and fork up against his empty starter plate. "Exemplary stuff – crisp, clean on the palate, a real triumph." He poured himself another glass. "So, back in the real world, are you much of a wine man?"

"Not really," I said, finding it hard, despite Gideon's loquacity, to feel anything other than thoroughly depressed about my predicament. "In fact, I'm not much of a drinker, full-stop. If I do pop into a pub, I'm more likely to have a pint of bitter."

"Oh, I see, that's interesting. I once had—" The dumb waiter clattered and dinged again, cutting him short. "Ooh, excellent, the main course." Rubbing his hands together, he pushed his chair back and got to his feet. "The suspense, the suspense," he said over his shoulder, walking across the room. "Mater never tells me what's on the menu, you see."

I watched him slide down the hatch, saw the mincing way he wiggled his hips and heard the little squeal of accompanying delight.

"Believe me. You're not going to be disappointed, old boy." He walked back over to the table with two enormous pieces of fish on two plates. "She *really* has pulled out all the stops – Turbot, king of the bloody sea!"

Over the main course and dessert, Gideon told me some disjointed details about his life, the books he'd read as a boy ("Hardy was my man. *Jude*, *The Mayor of Casterbridge*, *Far From the Madding Crowd*"), the gap year he'd spent travelling with friends ("was supposed to get that wanderlust out of the system, so I'd be ready to knuckle down at Cambridge, but it only gave me a taste for the high bohemian life"), his brief yet intense love affair with a pretty undergraduate from Yorkshire ("beautiful girl, inside and out, very serious, studious, though, had her whole life mapped out in advance. Whereas I...Ha! Funny how time passes, and you realise that your one chance at true happiness has already passed you by"), and how hard his father's death had hit him ("that bastard disease went through the poor old boy like a knife through butter, three months from diagnosis to a hole in the ground, didn't give the family a chance to really prepare".)

"I understand – losing someone close is never easy."

He looked across at me with glazy yet appreciative eyes, picked up his glass and knocked back the last of his cognac.

"There is something I've been meaning to ask you," I said, hoping he was sober enough to give me a sensible answer. "How do you live down here, all on your own? And how come you haven't put on any weight, eating all these rich, calorific foods, night after night?"

"Oh, I have a system." He waved my words away. "I'll tell you all about it in due course."

"But what do you do all day? Have you got books stashed away somewhere? A television? A radio?"

"No books, I'm afraid, although there's plenty of paper and pens. Think Mater is keen on me becoming a novelist, penning a wonderful book – nothing would impress her chums at the Rotary Club more than knowing I'm an esteemed literary man (hiccup). And no idiot box or wireless, either. Mater won't allow it."

Two firm knocks sounded against the door.

"What's that?" I swung round. "Is she letting us out?"

"No, no. Mater is going to give us a good night story, that's all. Come. Let's go and sit by the door."

As if it was the most natural thing in the world, Gideon got up, walked over to the door, and sat cross-legged in front of it, like a child at playschool. Bizarre as this was, I found myself doing likewise, crouching down beside him.

"Good evening, Mater. On behalf of us both, I'd just like to thank you for a truly wonderful meal. The turbot was out of this world, it really was."

"Good," she said from behind the door. "Are you ready for your story now?"

"Mrs Forbes-Powers," I cried, desperate to tell her about everything that was going on in my life, desperate to make her see sense, "please, you've got to listen to me. At present, I'm involved in a high profile murder investigation, am the only concrete link between two horrific killings. You might've seen them on the television news. I—"

"Nigel, please!" Gideon slapped both hands against his thighs. "You can't disrupt story time like this. It's not cricket. It's not done."

"It's all right, Gideon," said Mrs Forbes-Powers. "Mr Barrowman has only just joined us; it's his first day. He doesn't understand the etiquette yet. Besides, if his obtuse telephone manner, broken promises, and crass unprofessionalism are anything go by, I wouldn't believe a word that comes out of his mouth." She clicked her tongue. "High profile murder case, two horrific killings – my foot!"

I felt like protesting, repeating everything I'd just said, but something held me back – probably a strong inkling that my words would be roundly ignored.

"Now, if you're sitting comfortably, I will tell you a very dark and troubling story, a true story about my life and time in Rhodesia. Be warned, Gideon. You will hear things about your mother that you may find very disturbing."

Mrs Forbes-Powers' Story

To grow up in a land so obviously foreign in every way gives a child a curious sense of displacement. For all its beauty and charm, breathtaking vistas and fantastical wildlife, Rhodesia never once felt like home. In many ways, from my fourth or fifth birthday onwards, I saw myself as an intruder, an unwelcome guest. And despite the deference the local tribesmen displayed towards myself and my family, I couldn't help but feel a real sense of resentment amongst them, that our presence here was not at all welcome.

We lived on a large farmstead, consisting of thousands of

acres of land, sprawling out over the wild African plains. Oft times we would drive for hours on end, and still get nowhere near to our land boundaries. At the time, my father was in partnership with his brother-in-law, Humphrey Montfort, the competent if somewhat wayward husband of my Aunt Eliza. They, like my parents, were mother and father to an only child, a slightly slow, mentally deficient boy, my cousin and playmate, Charles. A rich fertile land, possessed of huge mineral wealth, our families combined to appropriate great fortunes from the Rhodesian earth. Within a generation, we were very rich people indeed.

Educated at home by a personal tutor, Charles and I spent the majority of our free time roaming the woodland abutting the nearby river, not a stone's throw from the main house. To ensure our safety, we were always accompanied by a few local children, "the savages" or "the little nigger boys", as my father called them. Half-naked, shoeless, these children nevertheless used to frolic around with such carefree abandon it made me feel left out, reserved and stuffy, as if I couldn't really, properly enjoy myself to the full, have fun like them, be a child, and deep down, I envied them their freedom. One boy in particular, however, Bunthu was his name, revolted me. Victim of an exacting childhood illness, the boy was hideously ugly, had what I could only describe as a brutal harelip, which exposed his fleshy gums and crooked teeth, his glazy eyes were always covered with a sickly-yellow film, he had a deformed hand, more like a claw, the arm of which he always held tightly to his side. Such was the repellent nature of his appearance, his own people used to tease and torment him. In the summer months, to amuse themselves, when the heat was incredibly oppressive, the nigger boys would play a cruel not to say incredibly foolhardy game of chicken with the river side alligators. Grabbing Bunthu's arms, two boys would drag him down close to the water's edge, where the fearsome reptiles had been known to attack people, striking without warning, clasping their victims in their jaws, and dragging them to a watery grave. From a safe distance, Charles and I would watch this sadistic game, laughing at Bunthu's pathetic cries for help. And ashamed as I am to admit it, I was almost disappointed when the alligator's snapping jaws just missed his trembling body, when the other boys pulled him away a fraction of a second before the lunging reptile could strike.

But this was nothing compared to the awful injustice I perpetrated against young Bunthu myself.

One evening, while enjoying a long lazy dinner outside, alfresco as it were, I did something so disgraceful and out of character, it would impact upon me for the rest of my life. At some point during the meal, I excused myself, requesting to use the water closet. As I walked through my aunt and uncle's part of the main house, I passed the master bedroom, the door of which was wide open. On a fine mahogany dressing-table was Eliza's jewellery box, like the door, open, as if she had been deliberating over which set of earrings or what particular necklace to wear for dinner. In one of the silk-lined compartments was a ruby brooch, one of the most beautiful trinkets I had ever seen. Unable to resist, I slipped inside the room, took the brooch from the box and fastened it to my blouse. Before the mirror, I performed a few shuffling balletic turns, right and left, hands on hips, admiring my reflection, the way the fading sunlight that filtered through the main window reflected off the ruby-red stone. So taken was I by this wonderful adornment, I couldn't bear to be parted with it. More than once, I unfastened the brooch and put it back in the box, exactly as I had found it, only to race back into the room and stow it away in my pocket. Conscience pricked, knowing that taking the brooch was very wrong, I did, nevertheless, steal it.

Early next morning, when I entered the kitchen, my parents were deep in conversation.

"Fiona," my father said with an unusually stern edge to his voice, turning when hearing my approaching steps, "yesterday evening, a very valuable piece of jewellery, a ruby brooch, was stolen from your Aunt Eliza's bedroom.

Now, cast your mind back, child, did you see any savages, the nigger boys, playing near the house last night?"

Heart beating fast, a horrible guilty feeling gnawing away at the pit of my stomach, I nonetheless told the cruellest and most preposterous lie of my young life.

"Why yes, Daddy, I remember seeing Bunthu out in the clearing, by the woods."

"I knew it!" My father slapped an open palm against the tabletop. "Those blasted savages! Can't they keep their hands off other people's property? No! We shall have to teach this one a lesson." He turned to my mother, who was then at the stove, preparing our breakfast. "I'll go and see Humph now. We'll drive out and visit the elder, demand the return of the stone, and the severest punishment possible."

Not just content with denouncing the wretched young creature, I went so far as to plant the brooch in the scrubland, near where I informed my father that I had seen Bunthu playing alone yesterday. This done, and for the rest of the morning, I felt a strange sense of relief, a curious lightness of spirit, as if I had exonerated myself, transferring the guilt onto the unfortunate Bunthu, who nature had already treated so accursedly, that I had undone a great wrong, because I was superior, so much better than that disfigured, deformed savage, that I had, in short, done what was only right and proper.

Early that afternoon, my father returned to the house, in a distant, prickly mood.

"What is it?" asked my mother – I could hear her from my bedroom, where I lay huddled up in anticipation, eager to hear the judgment passed down on the innocent Bunthu.

"Well," said my father, "the good news is we've recovered the stone – right where Fiona saw that sticky-fingered young bastard skulking around yesterday. Bad news: the local elder will not hand the boy over to us. No! They say that they want to exact a fitting punishment, as if they are better administers of justice then their colonial rulers. Huh!"

"What's going to happen to him, then?" asked my

mother, seemingly as curious as I was.

"Later this afternoon, they're going to hold some kind of tribal hearing, where, no doubt, some woefully inadequate punishment will be handed down."

Although my attendance at the hearing was not strictly prohibited, I knew my parents would not have approved of me leaving the house to witness events, events that, as aforementioned, would have a profound impact upon the rest of my life. Accordingly, therefore, I complained of a slight headache and tiredness, retired to my room, only to sneak out of the window, and trek my way over to the tribal lands, a half a mile or so walk from our farmstead.

When I arrived, it looked as if some kind of verdict had already been pronounced, for Bunthu had been taken to a primitive livestock enclosure, and tied to a wooden stake. In local tongues, of which I had no understanding whatsoever, one of the spirit doctors, face and body painted, admonished the captive, performing a jerky yet aggressive dance, while all the other tribesmen and -women mouthed words of sombre prayer. In the moments that followed, I couldn't quite keep track of what was going on (my vantage point, behind a tree, twenty or so metres from the enclosure, wasn't the best). The next thing I saw with any clarity was a stream of savages shuffling out of the enclosure, spreading out along the fence-line, two deep in places, like spectators at a sporting event. It was then I saw a fearsome boar being led inside the enclosure, a hulking, highly dangerous breed, native to the surrounding lands, an animal which often attacked humans, young children, especially, an animal which had been known to go so far as to snatch babies from cots. As if uncertain, the hideous, mud-spattered creature circled Bunthu, sizing him up, snuffling around by his feet and ankles. Then, letting out a rasping snort, it reared up on its powerful hind legs, arched its great neck, opened its fang-like jaws and tore the flesh clean from the young boy's face, literally stripping it away from his cheekbones, in the same way someone would peel skin from a chicken leg. Blood spurted everywhere. Again and again, the boar leapt up and attacked, sinking its fangs into Bunthu's body, devouring him in noisy, insatiable, frenzied mouthfuls. And how he screamed! How he howled in utmost agony. All the way home, tripping at every step, almost falling over, tears streaming down my face, all I could hear were those plaintive cries, all I could see was that rampant boar feasting upon Bunthu's helpless body.

A long silence followed.

"But – But, Mater," said Gideon, "you can't blame yourself for the boy's death. You were only a young child; you didn't know any better. Besides, how were you supposed to know that his own kinfolk would act so cruelly?"

"You don't understand," said Mrs Forbes-Powers. "That very evening, I was visited by a dark spirit, in the form of a horned owl, the very representation of which now hangs on your wall, watching over you. Late at night it bashed into my bedroom window, time and again. When I pulled back the curtains to investigate, I saw two great round luminous eyes staring back at me, eyes which told me I would have to pay a great price for my callous untruths, that a mark of death now hung over me."

"A coincidence!" said Gideon, getting more and more worked up. "Don't believe in such superstitious nonsense, Mater. It's only natural for you to feel guilty for the part you played in the boy's death, but—"

"But, Gideon, the same owl visited me as my waters broke when I was carrying you and your twin brother. Seven days after the birth, he died."

Gideon gasped and buried his face in his hands – clearly this was the first time he'd heard the story. In the silent moments that followed, there were so many things I wanted to say, about the owl, how I knew of the legend, but before I could even begin to formulate my words, Mrs Forbes-Powers started speaking again:

"Then, the night before your father complained of stomach pains, the ones which compelled him to visit his

GP in the first place, the pains which ultimately led to a terminal cancer diagnosis, the same owl woke me from my sleep, bashing against our bedroom window. And – And I've never told you this before, but the evening you were due to call in to discuss your future, following your unacceptable behaviour at university, the horned owl appeared yet again, outside the kitchen window, its eyes as bright and malevolent as they had been all those years ago in Africa. It was then I knew I had to keep you safe."

"What?" Gideon lifted his head. "So all this, keeping me down here, has been for my own benefit?"

"Of course," she replied. "I may be many things, but I'm not completely out of my mind."

Chapter Eighteen

"You know," I said to Gideon as he paced around the basement, showcasing his exercise regime, his 'system' as he called it, "everything I told you and your mother last night is true – about the murders I've inadvertently become involved with. To make matters worse, my former partner has now gone missing. A couple of days ago, the police dug up some old diaries she'd written, mainly about my violence towards her, our supposedly abusive relationship."

"Really? Doesn't sound as if she portrayed you in a particularly good light, then."

"That's just it. For ten years, she recorded a litany of untruths, complete fantasies, lies, saying that I beat and abused her, when I'd done nothing of the sort. For the vast majority of our time together, we were truly happy, in love. And I never once raised my hands to her. So, as you can imagine, it's made the police look on me as a bit of a nutcase, an unreliable witness, with her disappearing around the time of the first set of murders."

"Not good," said Gideon. "But it's funny you should mention diaries, because I've been keeping what you might call a fictitious journal myself, an alternative history of my life had I not had the misfortune of being trapped down here." He broke off from his pacing, walked across the room, pulled up the bed covers and removed what could best be described as a thick, bound manuscript from under the bed itself. "Work on it has been a bit sporadic, but I started on the night Mater pushed me down those steps. In this version, I call round like the prodigal son, a beautiful girl on my arm. Why don't you read it? Might help stave off the boredom, until you get your own system in place." He handed me the manuscript. "No pressure. If you don't find it of interest, don't feel obliged to plough through it."

Gideon walked for approximately another hour, our conversation sporadic, despite me trying to coax more information out of him regarding our incarceration. He then did something very odd, well, perhaps not odd, but unsettling, overly familiar – he stripped naked in front of me, and, unabashed, lingered by my bed, making lots of chit-chat, as if to delay the hot shower he said he was looking forward to so much.

"I suppose this is something else we'll have to get used to," he said, "– undressing in front of each other, bathing, going through our daily ablutions as it were, bowel movements et cetera. Probably best if we avert our eyes and whistle a cheery tune. Ha!" He grabbed a towel from his bed and walked over to the washroom, saying over his shoulder, "Then again, I'm sure it's something we'll get used to."

As Gideon took a long-drawn-out shower, humming an irritating tune I didn't recognise, I picked up the manuscript and started to read from what he *said* were his diaries. And I express myself in such a doubtful manner because what I found was not a personal journal of any kind, but the opening chapters of a novel.

The Magister's Analects

1

Armed guards ushered the detainees into a squat grey building of only thirty-four storeys. The words Central Party Re-Assimilation and Conditioning Centre were inscribed above the main door, alongside the Party's revised motto: Stability and Identity through New Confraternities. Once inside, they were taken to the main processing room and lined up in front of an imposing, pony-tailed figure with elaborate moustaches.

"I shall begin at the beginning," he told them. "Since the Great Catastrophe our industrial output has dropped to an unacceptable level. Worker numbers as well as morale are

now at an all-time low."

He walked over to a ragged, emaciated detainee and made such intense eye contact, the prisoner had to look away.

"I am your Magister. Here you will display a capacity and eagerness to learn as if you were behind in your learning, showing fear of losing what has already been learned." He started to pace up and down. "The follies of the great demographers have left us in an unenviable position. As a result of strict family planning many of you have never known the intimacies of your fellow workers, past and present, the things that give a man purpose in life."

The Magister approached another detainee, a tall, proud-faced man who was in much better physical condition than the others.

"What's you name?"

"Ye Ting Fang."

"Why are you here?"

He was slow in answering so the Magister dealt him a blow to the head.

"I, erm...I don't know."

"If you don't know now," said the Magister. "You will by the time you leave here."

The other detainees exchanged worried looks.

Moving on, the Magister continued his address:

"The human heart is more dangerous than mountains or rivers, more difficult to know than heaven. Heaven has its seasons of spring, summer, autumn and winter, and its times for sunrise and sunset. But humanity has a thickly-coated exterior and its true nature is hidden deep within." He paused and adjusted the lapels of his silken robe. "There will be three stages to your reintegration. There is learning, there is understanding, and then there is acceptance. You will now be taken to the sanitation units where you will be shaved, deloused and disinfected. In the morning, we shall begin the first stage of your training."

2

Pale moonlight filtered in through the window of cell number sixty-eight. Ye Ting Fang lay on his bunk, staring at the indent in the mattress above. His cellmate, a scrawny young man with wire-framed glasses, shifted position, rolling onto his side.

"My name is Chun Zeng," *he whispered.* "And you are Ye Ting Fang. I heard you tell the Magister earlier. Where are you from?"

"Hubei province."

"Hubei province! You were there during the Great Catastrophe?"

"Yes. I was amongst an elite group of workers sent to assist with the installation and maintenance of the new turbines."

"Ah, you talk of the mighty Three Gorge Dam."

"That's correct. I was training to become an engineer. But not long after I arrived the rains started."

"The rains!" *Chun Zeng sat up.* "Who could've foreseen such a tragedy when water was so sought after?"

"Exactly. Now I realise that you cannot tinker with nature, no matter how clever or powerful you think you are, or how much scientific knowledge you acquire. Nature is unconquerable. Building such restrictive barriers to try and constrain her was a grave error."

"There were so few survivors," *said Chun Zeng.* "You must've lost some loved ones."

"Yes," *Ye Ting Fang said slowly.* "My – My wife."

"I'm sorry to hear that. I've never had a woman before, let alone a wife, so I can only imagine a small proportion of your pain. As the proverb says, how can the frog in a well discuss the ocean? Still, it must've been a truly blessed thing: to have had someone to love, a companion to receive your affections, to go through life together, hand-in-hand."

They fell silent for a few moments.

"I'm very afraid," *said Chun Zeng.* "Have you any idea why we're here?"

"No I don't, friend Chun. But do not fear. Fate has

brought us together, and from this day forward I promise to look out for you."

3

The sun rose in a pinkish plethora of fractured sky. A convoy of giant hover vehicles rumbled into the main compound, parking close to the processing room. In pairs, guards unloaded the contents from the storage facility of each vehicle. From the doorway, the Magister supervised the delivery, his thick, plaited ponytail hanging limply from the back of his head.

Two guards dropped a bulky container.

"Careful, you imbeciles!" the Magister shouted. "This apparatus is crude enough without you wantonly damaging it!"

They picked up the container, stacked it, kowtowed, and scuttled away.

"Your Excellency!" A chubby, red-faced cadre in a military tunic rushed over. "I've just checked the consignment, and am happy to report that all requested items have arrived intact."

"The lubrication oil has been stored at the correct temperature, and in the correct manner?"

"Yes, Your Excellency. I personally oversaw each drum being deposited into the storage room."

"Very good, Hui Tzu. You have performed adequately. After the morning briefing we will select a pair of detainees to trial the new equipment. I'll leave it to your discretion. For now, you are dismissed."

4

The detainees, shorn of all their hair, and wearing bright-orange overalls, were marched back into the processing room, where armed guards lined them up in front of the Magister.

"I suppose you are wondering what you are doing here?" Once again, he started pacing up and down. "You are now my pupils. And do not think that I will conceal

anything from you. I do not act without my pupils. But I need you to be aware of four things; four rules, if you will. I allow for no speculation, no absolute definitude, no inflexibility, and no, I repeat, no selfishness."

The detainees looked on confusedly.

"You, the workers, are not unlike the mystical oak trees found in the old fables. Your number is limitless, your uselessness unbounded. Here, I will transform you into functioning citizens. For how can a carriage move without its yoke bar?" Turning to some functionaries standing by the exit, the Magister shouted, "Hui Tzu."

He rushed over.

"Yes, Your Excellency."

"Did you select our guinea pigs?"

"Most certainly, Your Excellency."

"Good. I'll prepare the equipment. Give them the prescribed injections, and then bring them to me. Be prompt in your action."

"As you wish, Your Excellency."

Hui Tzu looked on as his master walked out of the room, before turning to face the detainees.

"Ye Ting Fang and Chun Zeng, from cell number sixty-eight. Come with me. The rest of you are dismissed. You will not be needed until tomorrow."

The chosen detainees were taken to a harshly-lit, white-padded cell, empty save for a long metal bench that resembled the frame of a bed, with elaborate modifications at either end.

"As you are no doubt aware," said the Magister, walking across the cell to meet them, "the Imperialist powers are closing in. We must, therefore, reinvigorate our workers, providing each with emotional and physical companionship." He paused for a moment and smoothed down his moustaches. "So let me put a question to you. Were either of you married?"

No response.

"Answer!" A guard lunged forward, threatening to strike them.

"I was once married," said Ye Ting Fang.

"And you remember how good it felt to be loved?" asked the Magister. "Such intimacies can make a man into an even better man. Don't you agree?"

Ye Ting Fang nodded.

"From this day forward, therefore," said the Magister, "you mustn't consider each other as men. You are workers, working towards a clearly defined goal. No more, no less. And when all is said and done, a sexual act is merely a sexual act, exclusive of traditional conception."

"What are you suggesting?" said Ye Ting Fang.

"For the future of our society, we want each worker to provide compassion and relief for his fellow worker. This will be achieved by same-sex relations. Here, my pupils, you will be schooled in ways of gratifying each other."

"What? Never!" cried Ye Ting Fang. "It would be sacrilegious to my wife's memory! I would sooner die."

"Your courage is commendable," said the Magister, "but insufficient by itself. Don't you know the story of the praying mantis? In its anger it waved its hands in front of a speeding carriage, having no understanding that it could not stop the carriage, but having full confidence in its own powers. Be on guard! Be careful! If you are enraged with baseless pride you will face a similar fate."

Chun Zeng made a clumsy grab for his cellmate's hand.

"But I don't want to die."

"You so much want to live"—Ye Ting Fang turned to face him, "that you're prepared to subject yourself to such abominations? You're—"

"Guards!" the Magister shouted. "Strip them." He pointed to Ye Ting Fang. "Take this one over to the treatment bench. I think we've selected our first receiver."

Both detainees were stripped of their overalls. The bones protruded sharply from Chun Zing's wasted body. In contrast, Ye Ting Fang was lean and muscular.

The Magister walked over to the metal structure.

"Here is the training bench. It is completely covered for your comfort." Walking around the bench, he picked up a

set of straps. "Here are straps for the hands, feet and neck, to bind the receiver fast – an interim measure, until you familiarise yourselves with the apparatus. At the top of the bench, where the receiver lays down first, is a little gag of felt, which goes straight into his mouth. It is meant to keep the receiver from screaming or biting his tongue." He stopped pacing. "Right, for your first instruction, we must learn how to prepare ourselves."

He clapped his hands.

A small hooded figure entered the cell, knelt by Chun Zeng, and proceeded to fellate him.

"Note the technique," the Magister said to Ye Ting Fang. "This oral method of stimulation achieves best results for maximum arousal."

Knees almost buckling, Chun Zeng moaned with pleasure.

After a moment or two had passed, the Magister ordered the hooded figure to leave the room, and then told the guards to strap Ye Ting Fang to the bench.

"Remember," said the Magister, chuckling to himself. "Abed, do not stretch out in repose."

When the guards had secured the straps, the Magister applied some lubrication oil to Ye Ting Fang's anus. The guards then helped Chun Zeng up onto the bench.

"Oh, and don't worry about any infections," the Magister told them. "You've both been given suitable antiviral injections. Go ahead, insert, do anything you want. Think the gentleman is no more than an implement."

Taking Chun Zeng's erect member, a guard guided it into Ye Ting Fang, the lubrication oil allowing the penis head to slip in with ease.

"He is yet to enter the inner chamber," said the Magister. "But he has indeed ascended to the hall."

The guard pushed Chun Zeng backward and forward.

"That's it," the Magister encouraged.

Chun Zeng began to shake and murmur. The receiver buried his face deep in the covering, biting down on the piece of felt.

Letting out a cry, Chun Zeng ejaculated, bursting into floods of tears, collapsing against Ye Ting Fang, planting wild kisses to his back and shoulders.

"Excellent," said the Magister. "But leave him now. Colour rendering comes after the sketching."

One guard removed Chun Zeng; others unfastened the bindings from Ye Ting Fang's wrists, ankles and neck.

"Before moving him," said the Magister, "apply the jet device to the orifice and swill out the arising fluid. Then we can reverse the roles. And remember, my pupils, to learn without thinking is labour in vain. To think without leaning is desolation!"

"How far have you got?"

I gave a start.

Gideon was leaning over my shoulder, water dripping from his hair and still naked body – which, considering what I'd just read, made me leap up, off, and away from the bed.

"Sorry. I didn't mean to sneak up on you, to make you jump."

"No, no, that's okay," I lied, tossing the manuscript aside. "Only what you gave me to read wasn't your journal but the opening chapters of a novel, *The Magister's Analects*."

He assumed a shocked expression, one that wasn't totally convincing.

"Did I? Damn. Must've handed you the wrong manuscript by mistake." He hesitated, his eyes darting from side to side. "And, erm…what did you think, of the story, I mean? A little—" The dumb waiter rattled and dinged. "Oh, excellent." He walked across the room. "No doubt Mater has just sent me down some fresh togs."

He opened the dumb waiter and took out a pile of pressed laundry.

"Just the ticket," he cooed, stepping into a pair of brilliant-white bikini briefs. "Can't beat a good hose-down and some nice clean clothes, what?" He slipped his arms into another smart button-down shirt. "Are you, erm…going to jump into the shower now, Nigel?"

"Oh, no, no," I blurted out. "I think I'll, erm…wait until later, before dinner."

Chapter Nineteen

"Last night," I said to Gideon at lunch, "what unsettled me most was your mother's story about the horned owl, because, as I said before, a horned owl shape had been carved into the stomachs of the hotel room murder victims."

He took a sip of chilled Chablis.

"Not to be evasive, Nigel, but I don't think we should broach such controversial subject matter. After everything Mater said yesterday, regarding your trustworthiness, I don't know what to believe. You might be making the whole thing up just to try and turn me against her. Besides, what are the chances of two people having two different stories about the same horned owl, decades apart? It just doesn't sound credible."

I tried to argue, to put my case across in a calm, logical manner, once again telling him about everything that had happened to me over the last week or so, trying to make him see what a terrible mistake his mother had made, pushing me down those steps and locking me up in this basement, the dire ramifications of which could endanger further lives.

"Mater never makes mistakes. It wouldn't surprise me if she'd looked into your background, your personal history, found out that you were a single man, a bit of a loner, and decided you'd be an ideal companion for me down here."

"Ideal companion?" I repeated, the story of the two detainees from *The Magister's Analects* rising to the forefront of my mind again. "Come on, Gideon, this is ridiculous. We're both being kept here against our will. Surely our only course of action is to try and reason with your mother. And if she won't see sense, then we have to attempt an escape."

"That's not going to happen, Nigel. I think you better

start getting used to the idea. From hereon out, it's just me and you, down here, together, making the best of things, helping each other through in any way we can."

While Gideon took a post-lunch catnap, I crept across the room and examined the dimensions of the dumb waiter. While not particularly tall, it was deep and wide, a space that could, at a push, accommodate a person of my height and build, if I somehow managed to crawl myself up into a tight ball. Once up in the kitchen, jumping out and overwhelming a woman of Mrs Forbes-Powers' age shouldn't prove particularly difficult. All I had to really worry about was subduing, or getting Gideon on side.

As I considered my options, I caught sight of something stowed away under the table tennis table, a plastic container, the words LUBRICATION OIL printed down one side. In equal measure, this shocked and revolted me. Like life mirroring art, I started to seriously suspect (and who wouldn't, in the circumstances?) that Gideon had some very depraved plans for me down here. In dread fear of the truth, I had visions of him spiking my evening drinks and performing all kinds of perverted acts on my unconscious body.

"Not to keep going on about it," said Gideon, "but, just out of interest, what did you, erm…make of the few chapters you read?"

"Erm, an interesting concept, the ramifications of Chinese population control, men being forcibly put into same-sex relationships."

Gideon almost blushed, as if he'd rather I hadn't picked up and read from the manuscript in the first place, despite that clearly being his intention.

"Oh that. Yes. Saw a fascinating documentary on the television, put the idea into my head. I mean, what can a man do if there are simply not enough females to go around? As the incomparable Donne put it, 'No man's an island'. And we all need a little bit of warmth and affection in our lives, what?"

His words as much as the hopeful way he looked at me were seriously unnerving.

"I wonder what's going on in the real world," I said, changing the subject. "If we really are stuck down here for the foreseeable future, do you think we could persuade your mother to give us a little information? I'm desperate to know how the investigation into the murders is progressing. I'm desperate to know if my girlfriend is all right."

Gideon, refreshed and far more amiable after his sleep, didn't, as I assumed he would, immediately dismiss the idea.

"No harm in asking. Mater might've stepped over the line, locking us up like this, but she's still got all her faculties. I'm sure she wouldn't mind relaying the headline news, giving you an idea of what's going on in the outside world."

When we'd finished eating and tidied away, Mrs Forbes-Powers once again descended to the bottom of the concrete steps outside the reinforced door. Only tonight, before she could launch into another story, I told her that Gideon had something he wanted to ask. But despite my prompting whispers, he refused to broach the subject of the outside world, the murders, to ask her to bring a newspaper down, to peruse the headlines, to update me on what had happened since yesterday afternoon.

"What's all that whispering about?" she asked.

Ignoring Gideon's scowl, I said, "Mrs Forbes-Powers, please, I'm desperate for some information about the murder case. If at all possible, could you check today's newspaper for any details?"

"Tut, okay, okay," she grumbled. "I'll go and fetch the *Telegraph*, see if there's any mention of this killing spree you keep referencing."

A minute or two later, she returned, rustling what was presumably today's *Daily Telegraph*.

"Here we are." She coughed and cleared her throat. "On page eight, there's a short piece that mentions your disappearance."

Police fear for the well-being of low-ranking civil servant, Nigel Barrowman. Barrowman, 29, of Ilford, Essex, went missing yesterday afternoon, and no one has seen or heard from him since. Police are especially keen to contact Barrowman as he has been assisting with their inquiries into serious criminal activities, including the disappearance of former friends, Mr Jeffrey Fuller and Miss Michelle Rouse.

"That's it? There's no mention of the murders or any leads or arrests?"

"No, no," she said. "Just concern for your whereabouts, I'm afraid."

Chapter Twenty

In the early hours of the morning, I heard Gideon's bed sheets rustle and his bare feet pad across the stone floor. Having been far too anxious to sleep, I waited until he crept right over to my bed, pulled back the covers and tried to climb in alongside me.

"What are you doing?" I swung round and pushed him roughly to the floor–which he hit with a pretty resounding thud.

I switched on the bedside lamp. To my horror, he was laying in a tangle of his own naked limbs, fully aroused.

"Nothing, nothing." He tried to cover himself with his hands. "Sleepwalking. I must've done all of this in a dream."

"Dream! I don't believe you. Circumstances, like the lubrication oils you've been hiding away, suggest that you've been planning to accost me ever since I was pushed down here."

"Accost you! Don't be ridiculous."

"Don't play the innocent, Gideon. I think it's time I told your mother. I think it's time she knew the truth about you."

This visibly shook him.

"What? No! Anything but that. Please don't mention it to Mater. She wouldn't understand. To her, homosexual activity is up there with murder and child abuse. If she knew what I'd been planning, she'd—"

"So you admit it, then?"

His face almost fell in on itself, as if only then realising his mistake, what he'd let slip.

"You're a homosexual?"

He sighed deeply. "No. Not really. I'm just, erm…a bit frustrated, confused, lonely, having been locked up down here for so long. Incarceration can do cruel things to a man. It changes him. It makes him look at gratification in a different way. It makes him realise how much he misses the pure physical release following ejaculation." He got unsteadily to his feet, his hands still cupping his genitalia. "Before you came down here, I'd simply pleasure myself if I ever felt the urge to, you know... It became, along with my walking, an essential part of my system. Oh, I don't know, in my former life I would never have dreamed of violating another person's trust like this. Maybe I've fallen in love with you, your character, the warmth of your personality. That's why I can't control myself."

"Gideon, you're not in love with me." I took a deep intake of breath through my nostrils and slowly exhaled. I needed to calm myself, to be able to exploit the situation to the full. "As much as I sympathise with your plight, I'm not that way inclined, and feel very uncomfortable with the idea of you creeping into my bed at night."

"It was nothing. I just wanted to lie next to you, to feel the warmth of someone's body next to mine."

"Still, I feel duty-bound to inform your mother," I said, seeking to back him into a corner. "If she knew what was going on, she might feel very differently about keeping us locked up down here."

"It won't happen again. I'll try and control myself. I'll–"

"Assurances are not what I need right now. What I need is help in getting out of here. At breakfast time, I want you to help me climb into the dumb waiter."

"What? That's crazy. You'd never fit in there. It's too small."

"No it's not." I walked over, gesturing for him to follow. "Granted, it would be a tight squeeze, but the area inside is deceptively deep. If I could somehow manage to crawl myself up into a ball, arms pressed tight to my chest, knees tucked into my body, I think I could just about do it."

We argued about the dynamics of the plan, Gideon eventually conceding that I might just, at a squeeze, fit inside, but that the weight differential would be apparent from up in the kitchen, that his mother would, in effect, be alerted to some kind of anomaly.

"She isn't stupid, Nigel. Once the blasted thing starts to ascend, she'll notice how much slower it is, and she'll refuse to open the door from her side."

"Then I'll kick my way out."

"Impossible. If you crawl yourself up into such a tight ball, you'd never be able to free your limbs, you'd be like a sardine in a tin."

Regardless, I wouldn't be denied. Knowing the main door leading up to the steps was far too secure, the dumb waiter was our best, and only chance of escape.

"That's a risk I'm willing to take. I've been gone for two days now. All kinds of things could've happened in my absence. I can't wait any longer. Lives are in danger."

Incredibly, the task wasn't nearly as difficult as we had both envisaged. Once I'd managed to get a firm foothold, making myself as small as possible, chin tucked into my chest, Gideon was able to push me further and further inside the dumb waiter, right to the back of the shelf.

"I don't know about this." He peered inside. "I think we should call the whole thing off, just for today. I think we need talk things through, and decide what to do for the best." He forced his arm deep inside, as if to block the dumb waiter's passage, like an unwelcome stranger's foot wedged in a door. "Once outside, you might go to the police. Mater would get into a lot of trouble. I don't think I could live with myself."

"Move your arm," I whispered, fearful of Mrs Forbes-Powers overhearing. "I won't go to the police. You have my word on that."

Why the dumb waiter suddenly started to ascend, I never discovered. Maybe the old woman in the kitchen above had heard us arguing, maybe she inadvertently pushed a button in error, or maybe it was simply force of habit, whatever the cause, it began to rise with Gideon's arm still jammed inside.

"No!" he cried. "Mater! Turn it off! Turn it off!"

But it was too late, the ascending appliance crushed Gideon's arm, wrenching it away from the shoulder joint, until bone and sinews crunched, until he was screaming out in pain, until a dark claret stain seeped through his shirt, until the dumb waiter juddered to a halt.

In the chaotic moments that followed, where I desperately tried to get out, to squeeze my way past Gideon, whose legs by this time had started to buckle, to give way beneath him, I heard a key scraping around the lock, the handle turn, and the door clatter open.

"My God!" Mrs Forbes-Powers rushed across the basement. "What have you –? You fools!"

With admirable speed of thought, she pushed the down button, lowering the tray, which released Gideon's ruined shoulder. With utmost care, the old lady then slowly guided her son backward, easing his arm out of the dumb waiter. In turn, I pushed forward, squeezing myself out, close behind him, where I spilled to the floor. Not wasting a second, I leapt to my feet and, ignoring pleas of both mother and son ("Call an ambulance!" "You can't leave us like this! Gideon will die!"), I raced up the stairs. In panic, thinking of nothing but getting out of the house, I dashed down the hallway, turned the key in the lock, and threw open the door, the sharp morning air hitting me like a well-directed slap to the face.

No sooner had I rushed out of the house than a car raced over to the kerb, skidding to a halt. Confused, frightened, I looked on as a window wound down, revealing a familiar face, that of Bannister, the private detective who'd been hired by Michelle's family.

"Come with me, if you want to live," he said, like something out of a seventies cop show.

"What? Why? I—"

"Late last night, Jeffrey Fuller was found horrifically murdered. You're the number one suspect. Get in or risk being convicted of a crime you never committed."

Chapter Twenty-One

There were so many things I wanted to ask Bannister, I literally couldn't travel for a moment longer without at least satisfying some of them.

"Stop!" I shouted, banging a balled fist against the dashboard

Instinctively, he hit the brakes, jolting us to a sudden stop.

"For pity's sake! What is it?"

"I need to know what's happened? Tell me everything."

Bannister took a deep intake of breath, and slowly exhaled. "Okay, Mr Barrowman. I understand. But time really is of the essence, so let me précis events as quickly as I possibly can: the police were baffled by your disappearance, the only lead was the old woman you'd visited (the fact I turned up this morning, by the way, was completely by chance), but she said you left her house after about five minutes. Due to you going missing, all other members of your former counselling group were moved to a safe house. On searching your flat, the police found, amongst other highly incriminating evidence on your computer, a wooden box, a rare antiquity with a horned owl symbol carved into the lid. When they took it for D.N.A. testing, blood traces matching those of the deceased women in the hotel room were found."

"What? But my girlfriend, Liz, bought that box from Portobello Road Market, days after the killings."

"And that, to the best of my knowledge, is exactly what she told the police when questioned. But the stall-holder she claims to have purchased the box from has vanished without a trace. Then, late last night, Fuller's body was found in a field, cut up, just like the other three. All of which, since nobody could account for your whereabouts, has made you number one suspect for each killing."

I took a moment to take all of this in.

"What about Liz?

"Last I heard she'd been released on bail." He fixed his stern, implacable eyes on me. "This is serious, Mr Barrowman. The police have little else to go on, other than the theory of you being some kind of sick, twisted, psycho killer who's been dangling evidence under their noses from day one. In all likelihood, your girlfriend is now seen as an accomplice."

"But that's ridiculous." I leaned back and ran both hands through my hair. "Wait." I turned and met his purposeful stare again. "If that's the case, then why aren't you driving me straight to the police station?"

"Because information has come to light that suggests you're nothing more than a pawn in somebody else's game. It's imperative, therefore, that I take you to see Miss Rouse's parents. Everything will become much clearer then."

As if to emphasise the need for haste, Bannister sped off again, motoring down the road. Only he failed to notice a pedestrian, no more than a blur of thick winter fabrics, stepping into the road, and being sent tumbling up over the bonnet.

"Damn!" Bannister slammed on the brakes again. "Of all the…" he pushed open the door and got out of the car.

I followed after him, rushing around the bonnet, seeing the same woman from the supermarket and bus-stop, the one intent on securing fraudulent compensation for feigned injury.

"It's okay." I fell in beside Bannister. "I've seen this woman before. She does this sort of thing all the time: throwing herself in front of buses and suchlike, to try and get compensation. Chances are she's faking the whole thing."

But when we both crouched to examine her body, we saw blood pouring from a nasty gash to the back of her head, and that one of her legs had been broken, a piece of bone protruded through a thick pair of knitted tights.

"Oh no," I said, realising that, for the first time in her life, this woman had genuinely had an accident. "We – We better call an ambulance."

Bannister made a strange guttural noise, somewhere between a grunt and groan of displeasure.

"Not going to happen, Mr Barrowman." He grabbed my elbow and guided me up to my feet. "There's too much at stake now."

As if both thinking the same thought, we looked around, surveying the empty, deserted, early morning streets.

"I don't think I can do this," I said. "Can't we at least call for help and then leave? If not, she's going to die."

Rolling up his sleeve, Bannister showed me the tattoo of a horned owl on his wrist, the exact same owl I'd seen scraped across the dead women's skin in that hotel room.

"I think you know what this means." Yet again, we made brief yet significant eye contact. "Get back into the car, Mr Barrowman. Michelle's parents need to talk to you before the police do."

Bannister knocked three times, very deliberately, as if it were a prearranged signal, then turned the handle and walked inside the farmhouse kitchen.

"Hello, Nigel," said Mr Rouse, sitting beside his wife at the head of a long pinewood table. "I'm so glad you've been found safely. For a while there, we feared you'd suffered a similar fate to the others."

Despite Mr Rouse speaking first, it was his wife who did most of the talking.

"Please, sit down." She directed us to chairs. "As you're aware, Michelle went missing from her home over a week ago now. What you probably don't know is that Mr Bannister and Michelle were part of an organisation called The Horned Owl Society, an organisation that investigated cases of domestic abuse. Far more sophisticated than your average vigilante group, they have, over the last two or three years, tried to protect the victims and bring those implicated to justice."

Bannister glanced across at me, hunching his shoulders apologetically.

"Now, to give you a little more background information, both Michelle and Mr Bannister had suffered terrible abuse in violent relationships. Mr Bannister at the hands of his ex-wife, a vicious alcoholic manic-depressive, Michelle, allegedly at the hands of not just her former boyfriend, namely you, Nigel, but of her parents."

It took a moment for that last piece of information to register.

"Her parents? You mean you and your husband?""

"That's correct." Mrs Rouse picked up a bundle of bound papers. "Maybe you'd like to familiarise yourself with some of the allegations. All of which, I assure you, are completely and utterly false."

I took the papers and started to read from the top sheet.

Monday 27th February 1989

It just happened again. Mother and Father crept into my bedroom, semi-naked, with their bag of tricks, their handcuffs and torture devices. Time and again, I screamed and screamed, begging them not to hurt me like the last time. But Mother kept saying it was for my own good, that it would help me become a better person, a better wife in the future. No matter how much I struggled, how I kicked out my legs, or pounded my fists against Father's chest, it was no use – he was far too strong. Like before, they stripped me naked, bound my wrists and ankles to the boards at the head and foot of the bed, and performed all kinds of perverted sex acts upon me: inserting painful objects inside me, whipping my back and buttocks until welts rose, and making small incisions into the fleshy parts of my skin with razor-blades. And just like last time, I got the impression that they derived very little sexual gratification from these horrible acts, more that they enjoyed inflicting pain, that they liked to see me writhe, hear me scream, watch blood seep from my various lacerations, that it was the power they could wield over me that was the most important thing.

Afterwards, Mother dressed my cuts, dabbing the wounds with disinfectant, whispering soft, practised words into my ear, words laced with stark warnings: "Remember, darling, no one will believe you if you tell them. Remember your medical history. Remember how often you've lied to the doctors in the past".

It's like I'm trapped in some kind of horrible nightmare. What am I to do? Try and kill myself again? How am I to escape? Cut my wrists? Swallow some pills? Who can I turn to? Jeffrey?

I couldn't believe what I was reading, not just because of the graphic, sickening nature of the events described, but because it had been written at the height of mine and Michelle's relationship, when we were at our happiest. Moreover, at that time, if she ever talked about her parents, Michelle couldn't have been more glowing, fuller of love and respect for them. Countless times, we laid awake at night, Michelle in my arms, saying how awful she felt, putting them through all the heartache, all the hard times, how she hated acting the way she did – the depression, self-harming, suicide attempts – because her childhood couldn't have been more idyllic, her parents more perfect and loving.

"She's actually claiming that you both sexually abused her? I..." I trailed off, so absurd was the idea I'd just verbalised.

"So you see, Mr Barrowman," said Bannister, as if it was his turn to pick up the story, "when I told you I was a private detective, I wasn't being completely truthful."

He went on to explain how Michelle had given him some papers, telling him only to open and read them should anything happen to her.

"When she went missing, I naturally opened the bundle and read about your systematic abuse of her. Disgusted, I toyed with the idea of having it out with you myself, so sure was I, considering the nature of the letters and diary entries, that you were involved in her disappearance. There are certain things, therefore, that I need to confess. The phone call to your office regarding Jeffrey Fuller – that was me. I needed to hear your voice, to try and work if you were telling the truth."

"I see." At that moment, something important struck me. "And this organisation, why call yourselves after a horned owl?"

"It was something Michelle had read about. She said it was symbolic of death. She wanted to scare people who'd abused others."

I nodded as if that made some kind of sense – but it didn't, none of it did.

"After looking into the matter, after monitoring your activities for several days, I started to seriously question the integrity of everything Michelle had recorded in her diaries. I started to wonder if she hadn't made everything up, why or for what reason I had no idea."

"Maybe she wanted to create an alternative reality. Maybe she wanted to have a reason for feeling so desperate and depressed, so isolated, for wanting to hurt herself, to end her life." I turned to Mr and Mrs Rouse. "Did something happen after me and Michelle split up? Did she have another breakdown?"

"Not really," said Mrs Rouse. "Well, nothing worse than before. But, in time, she seemed to grow out of her problems, to mature, to look at life as something that should be enjoyed. On her own initiative, she got some voluntary work at the local school. In the evenings, she went to teacher training college, obtaining a professional qualification. She got her own place. She had a group of friends, including Mr Bannister here."

I turned back to Bannister.

"And was your relationship with Michelle strictly professional? Or were you involved romantically?"

"Well, we—" His mobile phone started to ring. "Erm, excuse me." He got to his feet. "I better take this." He walked over to the window and answered the phone. "Okay, okay… I understand…yes…thank you for the update." He clicked the phone shut and turned back to face us. "That was one of my people. Looks like things have taken a turn for the worse, Mr Barrowman."

This barely registered, because in my eyes there was no way things could get any worse than they already were.

"The police have been called to the scene of your incarceration. Apparently, a man has had to have an arm amputated, a man who now claims that you were lovers, and that you attacked him."

"What?"

"Look," Bannister said to Michelle's parents. "I better take him to the police station now. Only when we clear this mess up will we be able to find out what has truly happened to Michelle."

Chapter Twenty-Two

"Okay, Mr Barrowman," said Watson, twirling a pen around in his fingers, "let's recap on everything you've just told us. The day you went missing, you visited the house of a Mrs Forbes-Powers, a woman who'd contacted your office regarding dogs fouling the pavements." He looked up from his notes. "We've seen the correspondence from the woman in question and checked phone records to confirm this. On the old lady's request, you entered the house to look at some photographs of the area. Once inside, she pushed you down some concrete steps leading to the basement. You lost consciousness. When you came round, you realised that you'd been taken prisoner, that you were being held under lock and key, along with Mrs Forbes-Powers' adult son, Gideon. Is that just about the gist of it so far?"

"Unlikely as it sounds, that's exactly what happened."

"In the basement, we found lots of, erm…what can best be described as homosexual paraphernalia – various lubricants, anal relaxants et cetera. Did you, therefore, as is alleged by your co-captive, enter into sexual relations with Mrs Forbes-Powers' son?"

"Not knowingly," I blurted out, realising, as soon as the words left my mouth, how ridiculous they must've sounded. "After the first day, I started to suspect that he might be planning to drug me, so he could take advantage of me during the night. He told me he'd been down there for two or three years, that he was lonely, sexually frustrated, confused. He—"

"Then why would he accuse you of attacking him?"

"Probably to protect his mother. She's an elderly woman. And despite her locking him away like that, there's still a strong bond between them. You've got to believe me. Look at the facts! The Deputy-Director told me to pay her a visit that afternoon, after work. Surely you don't believe that I called round, met her son, fell madly in love in the space of five minutes, and decided to move in with him down in that basement, do you?"

Kendrick told me to calm down, going so far as to fill a paper cup with water from the cooler in the corner of the room.

"Drink this." He handed me the cup.

"Look, Mr Barrowman," said Watson, "we'll be completely honest and up front with you. Hardly a word of the mother and son's story makes sense – it just doesn't add up. What we're really concerned with is the murder case, specifically the horrific killing of Jeffrey Fuller. As you well know, before your disappearance, he was our number one suspect. Now that he's turned up dead, killed in the same gruesome manner as the other victims, everything has changed."

The gravity of his words went some way to refocusing my mind.

"So, coupled with the fact that you can't verify your whereabouts at the time of each murder, we're back to square one."

"But I swear to you, I haven't got anything to do with the murders. You said yourself there's nothing that can link me to the crime scenes. I—"

"Not quite." Watson pushed a photograph across the tabletop. "We found this at your flat."

It was a picture of the wooden box Liz had bought from Portobello Road Market.

"Your girlfriend told us that she purchased the item in the days following the first killings. But don't you think it's a little strange, a little too coincidental, that the box, when tested, showed D.N.A. traces of the dead girls from the hotel room?"

I tried to look shocked, even though I was already in possession of this information.

"In your absence, we spoke to Miss Green. Her story

regarding the box doesn't check out at all. So, we're going to have to go back to the very beginning and work our way forward, all the way through to your whereabouts this morning, in the hours after Gideon Forbes-Powers alleges that you attacked him, and the time you turned yourself in at the station."

In excruciating detail, we covered ground we'd already covered two or three times before: where was I on the night of the hotel room murders, the photograph at the office, the phones calls, the diary entries, the letters. Throughout, imperceptibly at first, but mounting in degrees following each question, I realised that I was now very much a genuine suspect in the killings. The tone of the policemen's voices had changed, hardened. There were no polite thank yours, no let ups, just an avalanche of questions.

"On your personal computer," said Kendrick, "in your browsing history, we found links to many sites relating to the Native American legend of the horned owl. In particular, detailed diagrams of the bird in question, diagrams matching the markings on each murder victim."

"I'm sure you did. But if you checked the dates of those internet searches, you'd see that they were all conducted after the first set of killings."

The way both policemen stiffened in their chairs told me that this fact had been duly noted, that I'd just picked a gapping hole in their flimsy theory about me being the killer. Still, there were more questions, tenuous, probing, accusatory in nature, the same things repeated time and again, like skilful traps, lain to snare me, to get me to trip myself up. But things which only made me feel sharper of mind, wary, careful of every word that exited my mouth.

"That brings us on to this morning," said Watson. "Undeniably – well, a young man had to have his left arm amputated from the shoulder – some kind of altercation took place in Mrs Forbes-Powers' basement. To all intents and purposes, it looked like a freakish accident involving the dumb waiter. However, as we mentioned before, Gideon Forbes–Powers alleges that you and he were lovers, that you argued heatedly over some literary work, and that in the ensuing argument, you lodged his arm into the aforementioned appliance, with the full intention of seriously injuring him."

"That's not true! I was locked up down there against my will. Seeing the dumb waiter as my only hope of escape, I crawled inside hoping to get out via the kitchen. In trying to stop me, Gideon's arm got trapped. When Mrs Forbes-Powers came down to rescue him, I made a run for it."

"Still," said Kendrick, "that doesn't account for your whereabouts afterwards. If you'd have been kidnapped like you claim, surely you'd have headed straight for the police station."

I hesitated before answering. In the car back from the farmhouse, Bannister had told me that both he and Michelle's parents would back up my story, that they would produce the diary entries they'd previously withheld, that, in short, they'd do anything they could to verify my claims.

Therefore, I told the policemen exactly what had happened.

"Okay, okay," said Watson. "We'll talk to Mr Bannister and the missing woman's parents, to confirm this part of your story. But, in the circumstances, you could all be in a lot of trouble – absconding from the scene of a crime, withholding vital information."

There was a long silence.

"For now," said Kendrick, "let's review the facts as you've presented them to us. Let's look at what you're asking us to believe: a man with a history of mental illness walks into a police station one morning saying he's got information regarding a brutal killing, a photograph sent to his workplace, marked for his attention. Only the photograph has been mysteriously stolen overnight. He claims to have received anonymous phone calls regarding one of the prime suspects. Then the therapist of his former counselling group is found murdered in the exact same grisly fashion as the first two victims. This man then goes missing for two whole days. An antique box with traces of the original victims' blood is found at his flat, along with related links on his computer. While he's away, the prime suspect is also found brutally murdered. And then this innocent man turns up at the police station claiming to have been abducted, locked away by an O.A.P. in a basement with her homosexual son, who he may or may not have been having a physical relationship with. And now, to cap everything off, he tells us that he didn't come straight to the police station to report his kidnapping because a private detective, who's not actually a private detective but a member of a vigilante group fighting for the rights of victims of domestic abuse, just happened to be passing the house when he escaped, and took him to meet with the missing girl's parents, to discuss another set of fictitious diary entries."

I put my head in my hands. Having the facts relayed in such plain, sober, matter-of-fact tones made me realise how preposterous my story sounded.

"Finally." Watson slipped some papers out of another file. "At the murder scene, we found a strange document amongst Jeffrey Fuller's final possessions, what appeared to be a novel or memoir of some kind. In the hours since his body was discovered, we've had our creative writing people evaluate the manuscript. Here are their initial findings, a basic outline of the plot."

He handed me the papers.

The Therapist's Dialectics
Basic Outline of Plot

Two men, both highly unstable, delusion mental patients, are locked inside a padded cell. This, as the reader soon discovers, is part of an advanced form of treatment – ultimate transference, as it is referred to later in the text. Each morning, a therapist, a senior, all-powerful figure, like a minor deity, enters the padded cell and schools the patients in techniques to ease the psychic blockages which are holding them back in life. At length, he relays his philosophical worldview, in the form of wordy epigrams, all of which have some relation to their mental problems. To help them relax, to become more responsive to the programme, various injections and potent medications are administered. The patients are then encouraged to discuss their backgrounds, past problems, their fractious relationships with their parents, how they always felt starved of genuine affection, which led to serious self-esteem issues in later life, where they could never initiate any kind of intimate relationship. They are encouraged to shout and scream, to help release any negative energy. After this outpouring is over, the patients are then instructed to show each other a little affection. At first, this consists of hugging and kissing at an appointed hour, when waking, after taking their meals, when turning off the lights to sleep at night. As the treatment progresses, so does the required level of intimacy. Now they are forced to kiss with open mouths, to strip each other of their clothes, to caress and fondle each other's genitals, to perform mutual masturbation, oral sex. All of which ultimately leads to penetrative intercourse, the giver and receiver determined by the dynamic of their developing relationship. After initial resistance, each patient comes to rely on the other. The intimate moments they share, the warmth, the companionship, not to mention the blissful physical release that accompanies ejaculation, become special, a fundamental feature of their existence. In short, they seem to fall in love with each other.

I couldn't believe it. I almost dropped the papers to the floor. The plot was almost identical to *The Magister's Analects*, only the backdrop, characters and situation had been altered.

"Is something wrong, Mr Barrowman? Does this story ring any bells with you? And by that I mean, did, to the best of your knowledge, Dr Rabie encourage his patients to become involved physically. Did part of his therapy revolve around sexual relations, like the characters described in the story?"

"No, no," I said, not knowing how to even go about explaining the connection between Gideon's and Fuller's manuscripts. "That's ridiculous. And it's, erm...been a long day, a long week. I'm really tired, out on my feet."

"Understood." Watson gathered up some papers from the desk and slipped them into files. "We'll call it a day now. You will, however, be kept in a cell here overnight. Not only do we feel this is the safest place for you at the moment, but we'll need to talk to you again, first thing tomorrow morning."

I was too weary to argue, but not weary enough to refrain from asking a couple of questions that had been burning away at me ever since I sat down in the interview room.

"Before you go. What's happened to Liz? Presumably, you've questioned her in detail."

"That's correct. And we'll be speaking to her again in due course, maybe after her next voluntary shift at The Samaritans."

"But is she all right?"

"As all right as can be expected," Kendrick answered this time. "She is, understandably, very concerned about your welfare and–"

"When can I see her, then?"

"You can't," said Watson. "Not for the time being. With so much uncertainty surrounding your claims re: the wooden box, it would be imprudent to allow you to confer in any way." Both men got to their feet. "Until tomorrow, then, Mr Barrowman. Have a bite to eat. Rest up. We've still got plenty more to get through."

Chapter Twenty-Three

That night, in an ugly holding cell, I had the strangest, most unsettling of dreams. In this dream, I saw myself in the same interview room I'd been questioned in earlier. Only now, I was a policeman interrogating Bannister.

"Okay, Mr Bannister, now we know you weren't completely truthful with us, we're going to have to go back to the very beginning and work our way forward, from the moment your ex-wife starting assaulting you, through to your first meeting with Miss Rouse, involvement with the Horned Owl Society, and your ultimate investigations into her disappearance."

"Right. I see." He lowered his eyes. "Only it's not the easiest thing to talk about. Me: the big macho man, former special ops, a soldier who'd seen more than his fair share of action, being unable to control his wife at home. But that's exactly how it was. For the life of me, I don't know what went wrong with our marriage. When we first met, Irene was a very feisty, headstrong character, but I liked that about her. It showed she had what it takes to be a forces wife. The first few years were a bit hectic. We moved around a lot, were posted all over Europe. But, like I said, Irene didn't seem to mind this nomadic lifestyle. She made friends easily, didn't get too attached to people or places, or too down in the dumps during my long absences away on tours of duty.

"The first time she hit me, and it was no mere slap but a brutal, full-bloodied punch to the nose, I didn't know how to react. The argument had been so trivial, so commonplace, I can't even remember what it was about. Now, looking back, I suppose she was testing me out, testing the boundaries, how far she could push things. Perhaps she even saw it as some kind of twisted challenge, to dominate a man of my profession. Whatever was behind it, it caused a violent haemorrhage in our relationship, one neither of us could stem.

"Weeks passed without another incident or flare up. Then, just like the first time, almost completely out of the blue, she struck me time and again, pulled my hair, scratched my face, grabbed my genitalia until I literally had to beg for mercy. It was baffling – the way I let her assault me like that. Because as the violence worsened, I found it increasingly difficult to put up any kind of defence of myself. I don't know why. Maybe I became resigned to my fate. Maybe I realised that I could never raise my hands to a woman, especially my own wife. Maybe Irene seized upon the fact, exploiting my innate sense of decency. That's why the attacks became so violent and prolonged.

"Things quickly escalated. It got to the point where I found it difficult to mask the black eyes, the split lips, the ugly gashes. I ran out of excuses: bumping into inanimate yet evidently vindictive objects, or trapping my hand in a car door."

Moving on, I asked Bannister how he'd met Michelle.

"At a meeting for victims of domestic abuse. I—"

"Wait." I raised a hand, gesturing for him to stop talking. "This could be important, a point that needs clarifying. If you met Michelle at such a meeting, and if the diaries and letters are, as we now believe, false, this is another indication of the lengths she went to to play out the role of the victim, to convince herself that she had actually been abused by her former lover and parents."

"Exactly," said Bannister. "Because of all the attendees, Michelle was the only one who didn't break down and cry."

"Didn't that in itself make you suspect that she was perhaps fabricating the story?"

"No, no, not at all. In my experience, different people deal with different situations in different ways. Being so brave and articulate could just have been her own unique coping mechanism."

"Okay. That sounds fair enough. But how did you become friends? Did you just get talking after a meeting?"

"More or less. In fact, it was Michelle who approached me, taking me aside, saying she felt great empathy, that it couldn't have been easy for a man to get up and admit to all those things, and that if I wasn't doing anything later, would I like to go and have a drink, so we could talk some more."

"And how long before she mentioned the Horned Owl Society?"

"Not long. About thirty minutes. Aware of my military background, she said I'd be the ideal person to help get the organisation up and running."

"And what was your original mission statement?"

"To name and shame abusers, to offer help and support to the victims – only with no, and Michelle couldn't emphasise the point enough, violence. Already she'd compiled a pretty comprehensive database; the names and addresses of alleged or convicted abusers. That's where I came in."

"How do you mean?"

"Well, with my training, the task of, for the want of a better expression putting the frighteners on someone, wasn't particularly difficult."

"I see. But how far would you go, bearing in mind that the organisation was to remain non-violent."

"We'd start by sending the abuser a photo-shopped picture of themselves, faces bloodied and bruised, mirroring that of their victims. These we usually blew up to A3 size, just for impact. Along with the photograph, we'd include a copy of *The Legend of the Horned Owl*, a Native American fable about a child born with the mark of death hanging over him, and the lengths his father goes to protect him."

"To indicate a revenge motif?"

"Exactly. Only the people we invariably targeted were of incredibly low intelligence, and this went right over their heads; it didn't have the desired effect. Realising this, I started visiting their homes at night, with a mock-up owl, no more than a puppet on a pole, which I would bash into their bedroom windows, scaring the wretched abusers out of their minds."

"And at this stage, did that constitute the entire scope of your organisation's objectives –campaigns of petty harassment?"

"No, no. We put posters up in town centres, in shops, listing the abuser's crimes. We put flyers through letter-boxes, warning local people. We made sure any abuser knew that we knew what they were all about. And in terms of results, we forced these bastards with potential to abuse again out into the open."

I hesitated before asking my next, crucial question.

"And during this period, I'm presuming you and Miss Rouse became close? You became lovers?"

Bannister shook his head. "We could never be lovers, only companions."

"Why not?"

Bannister gulped back some saliva. "Be – Because Irene, she took a knife to me one night, she cut me, between the legs, my – my…she physically emasculated me…"

Loud bangs sounded against the cell door. I jolted upright just as the bright overhead lights came on, the key turned in the lock, and Kendrick and Watson came rushing in.

"What?" I said, rubbing my eyes. "What is it?"

"Does the name Scott Richmond mean anything to you?" Watson almost shouted.

"Scott Richmond," I repeated slowly, a vision of Liz's psychotic ex-boyfriend rising to the forefront of my mind. "Yes it does. He, erm…used to go out with my girlfriend, Liz."

"Well, his body's just been found in an industrial bin round the back of the main council building, close to your office, in fact."

"What?"

"And that's not all," said Kendrick. "Disregarding the horrific injuries this man suffered prior to death, something had been shoved down his throat: a photograph of the original murder scene. Maybe the very same photograph sent to your office last week."

In a daze, I just sat there as they asked me question after question.

"And you say Miss Green arranged for a few family friends, who may or may not be part of the criminal fraternity, to pay Mr Richmond a visit, to warn him off, to stop him from harassing you in the future?"

"That's what she told me. But when they spoke to him, he denied having attacked me, and was so convincing, they believed him."

At this point, I was truly terrified. So many people had died, in circumstances so violent and bizarre, so random yet so obviously linked, I could see no clear way out for myself, so much evidence was stacking up against me.

"So what happens now? Surely I'm not being charged with anything. I was here, locked up, when the murder took place."

"But that's just it," said Kendrick "– no you weren't. The medical examiner who attended the scene has Richmond's time of death at approximately eight o'clock this morning, a good hour or so after you fled Mrs Forbes-Powers' house."

"But what about Michelle's parents and Bannister? Have you spoken to them yet? Have they verified everything I told you?"

"No they haven't. Because neither party can be contacted. It's as if they've vanished from off the face of the earth."

Chapter Twenty-Four

Whether I'd watched one American crime drama too many, it felt wise to request for a solicitor now. Every question the police asked was loaded, and I didn't want to risk losing composure and incriminating myself. Still, it was close to dawn before a legal representative finally arrived.

"No need to panic," were Julian Price's first words. "I don't think anyone in their right mind would attempt to prosecute on this evidence."

Even though he must've been disturbed in the early hours of the morning, Price, a tall, angular, well-dressed man in his early fifties, showed no signs of tiredness or irritability. In fact, he couldn't have appeared more alert, or better informed regarding the murders, my connection to the victims, and how I'd helped the police with their inquiries.

"From the outset, you've cooperated fully with the authorities." He sat on the bench beside me. "Now, let's break things down. Crucially, there's no physical evidence linking you to any of the crime scenes. So if the police suspect that you're involved in the killings, they must think you've acted as an accessory, the prime suspect appearing to be Jeffrey Fuller."

"But he's dead now."

"Exactly. So, by process of elimination, the only other credible suspect, the only other person not accounted for, is Miss Michelle Rouse. Which, neatly enough, brings us round to the diaries and letters, at best, circumstantial evidence against you."

"What about Michelle's parents and Bannister? Do you think they could be involved to some degree?"

"This is where we may face some problems: explaining your disappearance, the way you bumped into Bannister by chance, and the as yet unverified visit to the Essex farmhouse."

"But I swear to you. I was pushed down some steps and kept under lock and key. Everything happened just the way I told the police."

"And I believe you, Mr Barrowman. But it would appear that the mother, Mrs Forbes-Powers, has taken a turn for the worse, a minor stroke of some description. Being of advancing years, the doctors aren't holding out much hope of her pulling through. And it looks as if the son has decided to make a play at being mentally incompetent."

"Which means?"

"That neither mother nor son can confirm or deny that you were locked away in that basement. Although it's clear something highly irregular took place down there." He stared into space for a moment, as if mulling this particular point over in his head. "Then we've got the wooden box your girlfriend bought at Portobello Road Market, and the violent killing of Scott Richmond, someone not directly involved with your old counselling group, but a man who nonetheless had a photograph of the original murder scene on his, erm…person, when his body was found, indicating that whoever murdered him wanted to once again tie you to the victim."

"From what the police told me, it must've been the same photograph, the one that was originally stolen from my desk drawer."

"And I'd agree," said Price. "So, for the time being, we really need Mr and Mrs Rouse and this Bannister chap to turn up. They're the only people who can verify your whereabouts for the crucial hours when the latest murder took place."

"But they didn't say anything about dropping out of sight. I got the impression, well, Bannister said as much, that they just wanted to talk to me first, to show me the diaries accusing them of abusing their daughter, because they knew about the diaries and letters implicating me."

Again Price told me not to worry. Until I was officially

charged, which was highly unlikely, there was no point in upsetting myself unnecessarily. Legally speaking, the police could only hold me for another twenty-four hours. In that time, if they wanted to question me again, Price would insist on being present.

"At some stage today, I'll try and speak to your girlfriend, Miss Green. Undoubtedly the wooden box is a highly contentious piece of evidence, as she freely admits to having brought it to your flat." He hesitated before asking, "You haven't known her all that long, though, have you?"

"No."

"And you don't really know all that much about her background, either?"

"Not as such," I said, not really liking his tone or the direction the questions were heading. "But I seriously doubt Liz has been plotting and scheming against me."

"But you only really got to know her after you'd received the photograph at your office, right?"

"That's right."

"At this stage, then, with so many inexplicable events having taken place, I don't think we should rule anything out."

"How do you mean?"

"Just that, Mr Barrowman." He got to his feet. "Now, try and get some rest. With a bit of luck, we'll get you out of here at some stage today."

The duty officer hammered on the cell door, telling me that I'd got another visitor.

"Who is it?"

Surprise turned to disappointment when the door swung open and in walked Michael from the office, a thin folder wedged under his arm.

"Nige!" He shook me warmly by the hand. "So good to see you again, mate. When you went missing the other night, we all feared the worst."

As we sat on the bench; a uniformed officer stationed himself by the door, his arms folded across his chest.

"Caused one hell of a stink," said Michael, "– you going missing like that. By all accounts, the police had the Deputy-Director in for questioning. No one could understand why he'd sent you to see that old woman. It's not like dogs fouling the pavement are anything to do with Risk and Assessment now, is it? Then it turns out that they're previously acquainted, old friends of the family, and that she'd given him a right ear full about your attitude and telephone manner."

In between relaying chunks of information, much of which I could probably have guessed for myself, Michael moaned about his workload, how difficult it had been to man the office on his own, and how much he missed me ("not having you around is like losing a limb, Nige!")

He then took some papers out of the folder.

"And I know this sounds a bit cheeky, but could you go through a few of these claim forms with me?"

Strangely enough, I didn't feel outraged or offended by this, in the way most people undoubtedly would've done. I mean, in little or no time I could very easily be facing a multiple murder charge, and here was my line-manager waving some outstanding paperwork under my nose.

"This one here needs special attention."

It was then I realised Michael wasn't such a lazy, self-serving, self-obsessed bastard, after all. On the top of the pile was an envelope marked for my attention, not unlike the original envelope received at the office, only of a more standard A4 size.

"Yeah, if you could look at that one first, Nige, it would be a massive help."

As causally as possible, I peeled open the envelope and took out two sheets of paper.

The Revenge of Wapasha – A Dangerous Regression in the Narcissistic Patient

As discussed in a previous chapter, the Native American fable about the horned owl casting a shadow of death over an innocent child can relate to a patient's frustration when life spirals out of control, when they feel unable to alter their mood, when the complexities of their condition become too much for them to handle. In many respects, the mark of death becomes symbolic of a sense of helplessness. To counter this, patients should be encouraged to alter their myopic worldview, feeling as if everything revolves around them and their problems, to the extent that if some misfortune befalls them, however minor, they feel that the whole world is against them. Once the patient acknowledges that any individual is subject to the same random laws of fortune and misfortune, they are much better prepared to accept their fate in any given situation.

This was not the case, however, with the protagonist in the fable. After Wapasha's son is taken by the horned owl, he is subject to uncontrollable rage. He blames everyone else for his family's misfortune. When he returns to the settlement, he becomes involved in many heated arguments, culminating in one violent altercation after another, until he's ostracised from the community completely. Riding out over the plains, he goes on a murderous rampage, attacking a group of white frontiersmen, scalping men, women and children, an act which threatens severe repercussions for the rest of his people.

In an attempt to stop this violent rage from consuming Wapasha whole, Chief Antiman reaches out to him, telling of an ancient tale about a fearsome warrior whose father was murdered by original white settlers. To avenge his death, the warrior went on a similar murderous spree, slaughtering hundreds of sworn enemies, those that had killed his beloved father. But nothing he did, no matter how bloody or disproportionate, went any way to quenching his thirst for revenge. To save the warrior from himself, a wise man from his settlement rode him out to some old caves. Once deep inside, in pitch darkness, he instructed the warrior to ingest a powerful natural hallucinogen. When the drug took effect, and for the next three weeks, he sat cross-legged in the cave, experiencing visions both wondrous and terrifying. Only when he had had this ultimate showdown with self, with the rage burning inside, when his whole life passed before his eyes, when all of nature's wonders and terrors were shown to him, was he able to dispel the poisonous bloodlust, leave the cave and rejoin his kinfolk.

Antiman took Wapasha to the same cave and instructed him to ingest the same hallucinogen.

When he started to hallucinate, Wapasha became subject to similar wild visions, a tumult of past, present and future experiences, until he was eventually reunited with his murdered son. From cradle to grave, he watched him grow from infant-hood to boyhood, youth to young man. He saw the life his son would never live now, a life full of both happiness and pain. On each step of the way, Wapasha's dead son experienced all the things Wapasha and his own young friends had experienced, which reconciled him with the cycle of life, things repeating themselves ad infinitum, how each man and woman, every creature, animal, fish or insect was an essential part of things, whether they lived out a long and peaceful existence or died an early violent death. And it was this sense of his son belonging to the cycle, no matter how cruelly and unjustly he was taken from his family, which finally quelled Wapasha's own bloodlust.

This addendum to the horned owl fable is instructive in many ways, especially when one considers the connection between the ancient tribe's reliance on natural hallucinogens and the effectiveness of many modern prescription drugs in stabilising a patient's mood. In one particular case, I treated a patient – a very conflicted, angry individual, suffering from what I have since called the Wapasha Regression – who couldn't reconcile the anger boiling away inside of them, who could see no way out of their problems. This can be a dangerous phenomenon, one which can lead to self-harming, suicide attempts, or, as is the case of the Wapasha Regressor, violence, lashing out at everyone close to them. It is essential, therefore, that the patient be isolated and counselled one on one, that they are shown the unreasonableness of their thought processes.

This extract gave me much to think about. If Jeffrey Fuller hadn't been murdered, I would've assumed that the case study Rabie refers to was him. It all fitted into place: the angry young person struggling to deal with past events, i.e. the ambiguous sexual assault on his mother. But could this extract, now Fuller was dead, in fact have been written about Michelle? Was there something in her past that I didn't know about, were the killings, this whole complicated plot down to her?

"Is, erm...everything in order, Nige?"

"Yeah, thanks so much. I don't know—" Loud, agitated voices sounded down the corridor outside. A moment or two later, both Kendrick and Watson came rushing into the cell.

"Something's happened," said Kendrick. "Miss Green, in her capacity as a volunteer with The Samaritans, has been contacted by a member of the public claiming to be Michelle Rouse."

"What?"

"That's right, Mr Barrowman. Rouse has finally made contact, and she had some very interesting, not to mention very worrying things to say about everything that has happened."

Chapter Twenty-Five

"Like everything about this case," said Kendrick, "how Miss Rouse managed to contact Miss Green at The Samaritans is completely baffling. Each call goes through to a different volunteer at random, so there's no way she could've known that Miss Green would be manning that particular telephone at that particular time."

"Maybe she just tried time and again," I said, with little or no conviction. "Maybe it was simply a matter of trial and error."

"No." Watson shook his head. "It's far too random to even be considered a possibility. And the very fact that Miss Rouse knows of your relationship with Miss Green indicates that she, over the last week, at the very least, has been keeping a very close eye on your activities."

"That, or Miss Green and Miss Rouse are acquainted, and this is all part of a sick, twisted game, a plan to wrongfoot us at every juncture."

This I didn't want to linger upon. Twice in a matter of hours, Liz's integrity had been called into question. For now, I wanted to keep my former feelings towards her, as my only friend, my only true ally in all of this, clear and untainted in my head.

"And what did she actually say? Michelle, I mean. The interesting, worrying things you mentioned."

"Well." Watson glanced at a notebook open on the tabletop. "In a tone of voice Miss Green described as strange, unnatural, lacking the usual emotion in those making disturbing disclosures, Miss Rouse told of the sexual abuse she had suffered as a child, about her parents systematically molesting her from an early age. She then went on to describe the impact this had in later life, especially during her adolescence. In particular, the way her parents manipulated the situation, primarily with doctors, counsellors and therapists, branding their own daughter a fantasist, an attention seeker, someone prepared to embellish wildly, to make ridiculous accusations, to hurt herself, even, and how this ultimately made her feel like there was nobody she could trust."

Yet again, this information regarding Michelle didn't sit right in my head, because I knew how manipulative and deceitful *she* could be, I knew about her self-harming, her suicide attempts, and somewhat tenuous grasp of reality.

Watson resumed, "When the caller mentioned the rather unorthodox treatment she undertook with a certain Doctor Rabie, Miss Green realised something very wrong was happening, that perhaps whoever was at the end of the phone had contacted her for a specific reason, that it might, in short, be linked to the killings. Keeping her composure, she proceeded to ask a series of standard questions regarding the caller's life, about her friends and family, any treatments she might be currently undertaking, if she was on medication, what kind of support structure she had in place. That's when the caller started to get angry, nasty, confrontational, abusive, spitting out all kinds of threats and accusations, telling Miss Green that she knew all about her relationship with you, her arch tormentor, suggesting that you were somehow complicit in the abuse she suffered, that you were, in fact, part of a network of abusers who kept Miss Rouse as no more than a sex slave."

"But that's ridiculous! I didn't meet Michelle until we were both in our late teens, when we undertook treatment with Doctor Rabie. Any abuse she suffered as a child happened years before we became acquainted. The time lines just don't add up. Anybody can see that." I rubbed both hands up and down my face. "We were boyfriend and girlfriend, we moved in together, we shared a flat for years. And while we might not have been your average twenty-something couple, while we might've had our problems, I certainly wasn't involved in any kind of sexual abuse."

Watson and Kendrick shared a doubtful glance; the one that had unnerved me so much of late.

"But that's where the mystery deepens," said Watson. "In the course of a previous line of inquiry, we found that some of Miss Rouse's medical records were classified. On receiving the necessary clearance to view them – and this was literally a few hours ago – we discovered that there had been a history of sexual abuse, that, in short, Miss Rouse had been abused as both a child and young adult. Why this information was initially withheld, not one of our medical officers can satisfactorily explain. In light of this new information, we've put out an arrest warrant for both Mr and Mrs Rouse, and the Bannister chap, the so-called private detective, the man you allege was working for them."

This changed everything, not just about the ongoing investigation into the murders, but huge chunks of my past life, my entire relationship with Michelle, every moment we'd shared together.

"Now, Mr Barrowman, as I'm sure you appreciate, considering the nature of Miss Rouse's disclosures, we're going to have to take steps to ensure the safety of everyone involved."

"Safety? Why? Did Michelle make specific threats?"

"Indeed she did," Watson replied. "And in great detail. Referencing the fable about the horned owl, she told Miss Green that the mark of death was now hanging over everyone who attended the counselling sessions, over everyone who—"

"Wait! Why would Michelle want to avenge herself on a group of troubled young people who were in the same position as she was? If her parents really were abusing her, then why not just go after them?"

"Because Miss Rouse alleges that every member of the group was aware of the abuse she was suffering, that you all withheld information that could've saved her from years of agony. Therefore, she feels that you should all suffer, too. With that in mind, we're planning to move yourself and

Miss Green to the safe house the other group members have been sharing for the last few days. That way, your safety will be ensured. That way, Miss Rouse will be unable to harm you."

When the officers left the holding cell, I thought back to my relationship with Michelle, isolating certain moments in time and place, when she'd been upset and emotional, moments when she may've let her guard down, when perhaps she'd tried to tell me something important, but I'd been too blind to see. But there had been so many uncomfortable scenes, big outbursts of emotion, what I'd taken for crocodile tears, when Michelle had broken down, telling me about all the times she'd self-harmed, how much she hated herself, how she'd really, truly wanted to end her own life. Only now, after hearing such disturbing revelations, did I realise that nearly all her disclosures were about effect rather than cause, that all she'd confided in me were the various outcomes, withholding what was ultimately behind all those dark, desperate impulses. Were, therefore, her diaries and letters really a cry for help, after all? Because her parents, the people closet to her, had abused not just her body but her trust, had let her down so monstrously, she now associated any kind of affection with abuse, to the extent that she had to implicate anyone (and by that I mean specifically myself, Doctor Rabie and the rest of the counselling group) who had ever showed her any kindness or consideration in the past.

"Incredible!" Price walked into the cell shaking his head. "After everything that's happened today, now this Bannister chap has turned up out of the blue."

"What?"

"Yes. Just as police were arranging your transit to the safe house, he simply waltzes into the station."

Apparently, Bannister, after dropping me here, had called Mr and Mrs Rouse, to receive further instructions. Completely unexpectedly, they told him that Michelle had just contacted them by telephone, requesting an immediate meeting.

"By all accounts," Price explained, "Miss Rouse was distraught, saying that she'd taken things too far, that she wanted to turn herself into the police, but desperately needed to speak to her parents first, face to face."

Mr and Mrs Rouse then persuaded Bannister to lie low for the next twenty-four hours, contacting no-one, with the proviso that if he didn't hear from them after that time, to presume that something had gone badly wrong, to hand himself into the police, telling them everything he knew.

"Which, I'm delighted to say, includes a complete corroboration of your story re: your whereabouts following your escape from the basement. In addition, the location of the Essex farmhouse – the scene of which police forensics teams are at this moment painstakingly examining."

A huge sense of relief washed over me.

"And what else did Bannister say?" I asked, seeing him as the key to not just my own credibility, but many things regarding Michelle, because he'd clearly been closest to her right up until the time of the horrific killing spree.

"Well, from what I gather – and please remember, Bannister is still being questioned – the vast majority of his story, the information he's provided regarding his background, relationship with Miss Rouse et cetera, has checked out. There is clear evidence of him attending meetings for victims of domestic abuse, and of him and Miss Rouse setting up an organisation for the protection of those very same vulnerable people."

"And what happens now? What's next for me and Liz, for everyone else from the counselling group?"

"As I understand it, you will be moved to the safe house as previously planned. But, suffice to say, you are no longer implicated in any wrongdoing. Suffice to say, you are now considered a victim not a perpetrator or accessory in any crime. In a few short hours, you'll be able to have a shower and a change of clothes, you'll be able to walk around in relative freedom – well, at least you won't be encased in this windowless hole with its four lifeless walls, anyway."

Chapter Twenty-Six

On arrival at the remote farmhouse, I was led into a sprawling front room with exposed wooden beams and a roaring open fire. In each corner, standing lamps provided soft, subdued light. From either sofa or armchair, the women turned and stared at me. All appeared pensive, some smoked, others' held cups of tea or coffee. And even though there were few physical similarities between them – fat, thin, tall, short, dark or light hair – they were all strangely alike, in movement, expression, the way they held themselves, what they wore, even (although the dowdy cardigans and sweat bottoms had more to do with comfort than any true reflection of how each dressed in everyday life).

To try and lighten the atmosphere, I went up to each woman individually, shook her hand, and said how glad I was to see her again, only I wished it was in better circumstances – clichéd, granted, but sincere and appropriate nonetheless. Regardless, each one of them looked at me with utmost enmity and distrust.

Wendy, her plain, unremarkable face just as I remembered it, was the first to engage me in any substantial conversation. As she asked me about the original photograph sent to the office (clearly, all had been well briefed), I couldn't help but picture her at one of the counselling sessions, an eighteen-year-old girl sucking back the tears, telling us about her debilitating obsessive compulsive disorder, how it took her over an hour to leave any given room, for fear of having left a gas ring on or a tap running.

"As you can imagine, with so much time on our hands, we've gone over every detail of the case, analysing the evidence, looking at things from each and every conceivable angle. Helen and Riordan were gentle souls. It's painful to think of them being murdered in such a brutal manner." Her eyes darted right and left, as if seeking approval or encouragement from the other women looking on. "And it didn't really surprise us that you were the first point of contact. In the past, at the sessions, I mean, you were always the, erm…one person who channelled the flow, so to speak, who dictated things."

This was so contrary to the sessions as I remembered them, I asked her exactly what she meant.

"Well, not to be unkind, Nigel, but you were terribly forward back then, weren't you? your behaviour completely inappropriate, the way you went from girl to girl, trying it on, propositioning us, the way your groping hands used to wander, made us all feel very, very uncomfortable. Not to mention your outspoken views, on everything from the futility of counselling to an almost joyous endorsement of suicide."

The forthright manner in which she qualified her previous comments completely threw me. Even today, I remembered each session as being a torturous ordeal for me – a shy, withdrawn young man who rarely left his own bedroom. Only when directly prompted (and this could be an arduous verbal coaxing, Rabie asking question after question, receiving only a few fractured sentences in return for his patient efforts) did I ever speak to anyone. To be told, years later, that I'd behaved like an irreverent, lecherous, sex-fiend was not only shocking but patently absurd. It was as if Wendy was talking about somebody else.

"That's complete nonsense. It took six months before I felt comfortable telling anyone my name. For hours I sat in that poky little room feeling like a rabbit in the headlights. I —"

"Seriously?" said Cara, a tall, painfully thin woman with high cheekbones and porcelain skin. "Are you telling us that you don't remember the way you flirted with all us girls?

For the first few sessions, you spent all your time working on Helen, sitting next to her, carrying her bags, acting like an obsequious lackey, telling her how beautiful she was, how intelligent, laughing at any vaguely amusing thing she might've said. It was a truly awful spectacle, how creepy and fawning you became, primarily because it was so blatant, because everyone knew exactly what you were after. Even more so, when Doctor Rabie mentioned your masturbation problems, how you always liked an audience, and how you kept getting caught exposing yourself."

"What?" The incident she was presumably referring to, an excruciating episode at a local mental facility, occurred when I was trialling a powerful new anti-psychotic drug. To the best of my memory (and I had to be kept in full restraints for a week afterwards, a cloth gag inserted into my mouth to stop me from swallowing my tongue) was like an outtake scene from *One Flew Over the Cuckoo's Nest*. Wired up on the strong, wholly unsuitable medication, suffering from wild heart palpitations, more scared than I'd ever been in my entire life, I attempted to escape from the facility, having convinced myself that the people there were trying to kill me. In the ensuing chaos, one of the orderlies tried to chase me down, ripping a gown from my back. The outcome: me, fully naked, running around the ward, down corridors, out into the car park. Hardly a case of exposing myself, or masturbating in front of people.

"That's completely inaccurate. I wasn't ever– " But before I could continue, a woman I'd never seen before poked her head into the room and told us dinner was ready.

Over an almost unbearably tense three-course meal, the realisation that these women held me not just in contempt, for past deeds I had no, or a very different recollection of, but in some way responsible for everything that had happened only deepened. With thinly-veiled references and caustic asides, it was clear that they saw me as the catalyst, a Frankenstein to Michelle's monster (if she truly was guilty of such horrific crimes).

At a long table, we sat squashed together, an intimacy

that wasn't altogether pleasant or in any way welcome. As a result, I began to feel incredibly self-conscious, scared to move around too much, to lift my knife and fork, even, until every mouthful of food I put into my mouth felt taut with danger, a fear of bumping someone's elbow, of chewing too loudly, breathing too much. By the time the main course was served, I wanted to crawl up into a ball, to disappear, to be anywhere other than I was right now.

In the end, in an admirable if clumsy attempt to diffuse the situation, Clare, flame-haired, freckle-faced, a chain-smoker, one of the more distinctive characters in the group, then and now, banged her open palm against the tabletop, rattling the condiments and glasses.

"Look. We've all talked this thing to death." She turned and looked directly at me. "None of us were happy about you joining us here, Nigel. There's so much resentment towards you, so many things from the past which don't sit easy with any of us."

"Resentment?" I said, having difficulty controlling my voice. "I have no idea what you're talking about. I can think of nothing from the past that could have offended you so much. If anything, there were times when I felt incredibly intimidated by each and every one of you."

"Huh!" Cara spluttered. "That's rich. I don't know how many times you shouted me down during a session, how you mocked me when I was trying to talk about my problems, to express myself, to open up, to understand why I felt the way I did."

"But that was Jeffrey, not me. I never—"

"Oh sure." Cara rolled her eyes. "But only because you egged him on; only because you had him wound around your little finger. Don't think we didn't know what was going on behind the scenes – the way you manipulated him, turning him into your little puppet. Of course Jeffrey was the one who got into trouble, who irked Doctor Rabie most, but you were the one who planted all the seeds of discontent. You were the one who made all our lives hell."

Gloria, nervous, prematurely aged, a thick plait hanging

down close to her waist, shot to her feet.

"I can't believe you can sit there and lie through your teeth. First you pursued Helen, then Riordan. I saw you at work, firsthand, the time you cornered Riordan in a corridor, how you pinned her up against a wall and forced your hand between her legs."

"What are you talking about? Bar Michelle, Riordan was the only other member of the group I considered anything close to a friend. We used to talk, exchange books and compilation tapes. I would never have dreamed of forcing myself on her. Never!"

"But I saw you, Nigel," said Gloria. "And because of everything that happened, because you were so sleazy and twisted, we seriously thought you were the killer, that you were murdering each girl, in the order you molested them back then. Some of the things you used to say – the rape fantasies, the sexual violence – it made me sick."

This provoked my most vehement denial yet. Impassioned words flowed, arguments, counter-arguments, refutations, statements of facts, things which were irrefutable in my mind, things which proved I was innocent of all allegations, that I would never have acted in the way they were accusing me of acting. But even as I spoke, at the back of my mind, a nagging voice kept repeating: Why? Why would they make something like this up?

"And if you won't accept hearing this." Cara stood up, pushing her chair back with her legs. "Maybe you'll acknowledge it in writing, you own writing."

She stormed out of the room, returning two or three minutes later with an envelope in her hand.

"Here." She thrust it towards me. "Go into the study next door. Read it. Read it all."

I took the envelope and turned it over. A single word – *Cara* – was written on the front, in my own distinctive, slanting handwriting. Of this I had no doubt whatsoever.

"And when you've finished," she said, "maybe you'll have the decency to at least acknowledge and respect our past pain."

Chapter Twenty-Seven

It's hard to confront a version of yourself you never knew existed. But that's exactly what I was about to do – confront a different Nigel Barrowman, a stranger writing in my own hand, expressing thoughts I could neither understand, rationalise or condone.

Dearest Cara,

I thought it was about time that I told you how I feel about you. Every night before I go to bed, you are the last thing I think about. When I wake up in the morning you drift back into my consciousness like a blissful, angelic vision. I love you. And I know you feel the exact same way about me. During sessions with Doctor Rabie, our eyes have often met across the room. Your sweet smile is a truly wonderful thing; the way it lights up your beautiful face always sends a shiver up and down my spine. The two of us being together forever is written in the stars. All we have to do now is be brave enough to trust in each other. For believe me, the gifts true love, the joining of two hearts, affords, are the most exquisite imaginable. Sweet Cara, take the chance, grab it with both hands!!!!

Before I go on, however, before we make that heavenly leap of faith, there are a few things you should probably know about me. With trust and love, remember, comes complete honesty. When I was much younger, around ten or eleven years old, in the penultimate or final year of middle school (when you've been prescribed as much medication, and undertook as many hours of counselling as I have, times and dates become muddled in your mind), two very unpleasant incidents occurred in quick succession, which perhaps contributed to the worsening of my condition. Around this time, I started to develop, physically, much quicker than most boys of my age. By that I mean, I went through an accelerated, traumatic puberty, rendering me a full grown man, with fully developed sexual organs and adult desires, but without the requisite maturity and understanding to control myself. In one of my classes was what I can only describe as (and please forgive the crass, offensive terminology, but I assure you, in this particular instance it is as apt as it is justified) a filthy slut, an eleven-year-old girl, no more than a child, who wore short skirts, make-up, who was forever talking about sex, boasting of sucking boys off, of getting fingered or rogered, of doing all kinds of disgusting, depraved things, in and out of school. One break-time, some older boys attempted to teach this slut a lesson. In the most brazen manner imaginable, in full view of the younger children, she had been flirting outrageously, flashing these older boys her knickers, pulling up her blouse and showing them her surprisingly full, rounded breasts, even going so far as to grope their crotches, feeling their erect penises through their trousers. Like pack dogs, the boys, no doubt aroused, balls of pent-up sexual confusion, chased the slut into an adjoining strip of woodland. Curious, me and a few other children who had witnessed the scene, rushed over to see what was happening. In a clearing, a secluded nook, the boys had forced the girl down onto her back, and were taking turns, pulling up her skirt, clambering in between her legs, and thrusting away at her, ("dry-fucking" was the terminology the other children used), in effect, having sex with her through their clothes. Being young and naïve, this scene naturally captivated me, for each time one boy moved aside for his friend, I caught sight of the top of the slut's milky-white thighs. Her flimsy pink knickers had become twisted, sodden, wet through, showing wispy patches of dark, matted pubic hair.

When the bell sounded for the end of break-time, the boys and the other children panicked and ran off in the direction

149

of the main building. I, however, remained for a full minute, maybe two, watching the slut, dazed, breathless, but with a strange, tranquil look upon her face, eyes squeezed shut, legs still splayed, knickers down by her knees now, fully exposing her genitalia. Just as I was about to walk away, fearing she would see me and get angry, she moved her hand down towards her vagina, and started to touch herself, to gently stroke the strange mass of pinkish flesh, inserting a finger deep inside, as if exploring her body, her pleasure, moaning, perhaps experiencing something close to an orgasm.

Later than afternoon, when I returned home from school, I found a note from my parents, telling me that they had to attend to something, a family emergency, if I remember rightly, and that they wouldn't be home until about four o'clock. Since lunch-time, the image of the slut touching herself like that had never once left my mind. In English class, my favourite subject, I couldn't concentrate at all, to the extent that I received a mild reprimand from the teacher, Mr Hall, who was like a second father to me, an inspirational figure, a kindly, learned man who leant me some amazing books. With the house to myself, I rushed upstairs to my bedroom, stripped naked and began to reenact the scene in the strip of woodland adjoining the playground. And by that I mean, I crumpled up my quilt cover to resemble the slut's grounded body, twisted a fold of material around my penis and thrusted away in the same manner the older boys had thrusted away at her, grinding my hips up and down. Within seconds, I felt a tingling sensation, like nothing I had ever experienced before, and searing hot liquid jetted out of my penis.

At school, I had heard classmates discussing masturbation before, but had always avoided such base talk. Now I had experienced it firsthand, however, I wanted to repeat the sensation time and again. Picturing the slut's fingers slipping into her vagina, I desperately wanted to find something I could insert my penis into. Foolishly, driven mad by this freakishly intense physical desire, I selected a thick, two-litre, glass, Coca-Cola bottle, which I felt sure I could ease my penis inside, experiencing the tightness, the enclosure I so badly wanted to replicate. Perched on the edge of the bed, I tried to force the bottle over my penis, to squeeze myself inside, to work it up and down, just as I had a few minutes ago, into a folded piece of quilt cover. In my lustful impatience (and that's the only way I can describe such stupidity), I pushed too hard, too fast, too often, and the bottle cracked, the glass around the neck splintering, several jagged shards slicing into the top of my penis. The pain! The blood! The shame! The mad, mad panic! For no sooner had I gone somewhere close to mastering the shock, when I heard the front door open and my parents call up the stairs. A comical scene, I suppose, had I not been that stupid boy, rolling around on his bedroom floor, with blood spurting from his penis.

Suffice to say, I had no option but to call for help (and believe me, there was a moment when I seriously contemplated lying there and bleeding to death, just to avoid dealing with the situation, my parents, the ambulance, the hospital – all of which were humiliating in the extreme). And to this day, I still bear the scar from my imbecilic actions, a reminder of the dangers arising from sexual desire, when not strictly policed.

Hugely disturbed, I broke off from reading. Not simply because of the uncomfortable words I'd just read, but because I did indeed have a scar running down the tip of my penis. A scar, my parents had always maintained, which resulted from circumcision, recommended by a family doctor. But now, casting my mind back, I found it impossible to remember when I'd first noticed the scar – had it always been there? Or did I have some kind of accident? Did it just suddenly appear?

Frustrated by this memory lapse, a complete lack of clarity, I decided to read on.

As stated above, these two incidents, a crude, grubby sexual awakening, had a profound impact upon me. They created what I can only describe as a chasm, a gulf between how I saw myself as a sexual being and those I wished to engage in sexual activity with. In short, I had a skewed vision of lovemaking. I found it hard to distinguish between a consensual act and a non-consensual act – although that may be a clumsy way of expressing it. What I think I'm trying to say is that, for me, sex has, and will always be, about one person's search for gratification, not some spiritual coming together, making love, two people pleasuring each other. And if you and I are going to unite, Cara, I feel it important that you understand this; that you understand that you can have full possession of my heart and soul, the noblest parts of any person's being, but never my physical body.

In the aftermath of the two incidents described above, after my wound had healed, I'm ashamed to admit that I developed a fixation with the school slut. At break-times, I followed her around, I tried to speak to her, to make some, any kind of connection, because, in my undeveloped mind, she represented the easy gratification of sexual desire. An old, clichéd, commonplace phenomenon, I know, because many adolescent boys are drawn to girls of easy virtue, in the hope of gaining essential sexual experience. But for me it was different. I idealised this slut. I wanted her to see me as a kindred spirit, as someone she could entrust with her sexual favours. When she spurned each and every one of my clumsy advances, therefore, when she mocked and derided me, going so far as to shout, in front of a sizeable crowd of children, "Fuck off, Barrowman, no girl in her right mind would touch you with a bargepole. You're a fucking freak, smelly, ugly, a weirdo", I felt crushed. I became even more withdrawn, desperate, solitary.

From then on, there was always something voyeuristic about my sexual dalliances. Her cruel words had made me feel all the more marginalised, exacerbating my self-esteem issues, because I couldn't imagine any female liking me for who I really was, because I didn't feel like a proper or very appealing person, but the freak the slut had called me, abnormal, someone to be shunned and poked fun at.

Therefore, my fantasies, the things I used to think about in bed at night, changed accordingly – or perhaps it was more an affirmation of previous inklings than a complete change of mindset. Now all I fantasised about was an unconscious, drugged, yet fully living, breathing female lying on my bed, naked. That way, I'd be able to do what I ever I wanted to do to her, explore every inch of her body, without the risk of humiliating myself, of doing something wrong, so she wouldn't be able to judge me, look at me with anything like disappointment or distaste in her eyes, something I would've been unable to handle. So involving, so real did this obsession become, I started to devise various plans, ways of slipping something into the slut's drink, at a school disco, for instance, or a friend's birthday party. If I could just get her alone, I could exploit her body in a way I knew she would wholly approve of, in a way she could fantasise about afterwards. And here, I thought about perhaps filming myself taking advantage of her unconscious body, so she could play it back and touch herself, in the same way she touched herself after she was accosted by those boys.

So what I suggest, my sweet, darling Cara is that we both take yet another leap of heavenly faith. Let me put you to sleep with a mild yet effective sedative. In my room or yours, whichever becomes available soonest, we can seal our union; we can record our unconscious coupling, our selfish acts of pleasure, and play them back, time and again. That way, we will have an eternal testament of our love for each other. Think how truly special that would be!

In conclusion, I understand how strange, maybe even unsettling, this request might appear. But, and I can't emphasise this enough, I am fully prepared to go through the same process, the process of being drugged myself.

So, here I am in my room, awaiting your response. But somehow I know your mind is totally attuned to mine, that we are, to all intents and purposes, already a single living, breathing entity, two hearts beating as one.

Write soon, my darling, Cara. We have much to arrange – our whole lives together.

Yours eternally
Nigel

Two firm knocks sounded against the study door, disturbing my thoughts before I'd really had a chance to put them into any kind of coherent order. The brass handle rattled and turned. I looked over my shoulder to see Bannister walking into the room.

Chapter Twenty-Eight

"Ah, Mr Barrowman, the, erm…ladies in the dining-room were kind enough to point me in your direction." He looked right and left, grabbed a chair from beside the empty fireplace, dragged it over to the writing desk, and sat down beside me. "Firstly, let me apologise for slipping off the radar the other day. But, as I'm sure you're now aware, Mr and Mrs Rouse claimed to have heard from their daughter and—"

"Claimed?"

"Why, yes, look at the facts: classified medical reports confirming that Michelle had indeed been abused throughout her childhood, into her teenage years. In such circumstances, and mountains of scientific research backs this up, the perpetrators are nearly always close family members. And if that was the case, then perhaps the diary entries they showed you at the farmhouse the other day were genuine, and the ones found at Michelle's home were written under duress."

"What? So you think Michelle's parents sexually abused her for years, and then got her to write those diaries and letters, accusing me, just to throw the police off the scent, should anything ever come to light?"

"Maybe, maybe not." Bannister leaned closer, propping his elbows on his knees. "However, shocking as that possibility undoubtedly is, it's not, I fear, our most pressing concern at present."

"How do you mean?"

He glanced warily over his shoulder, before saying, almost at whisper, "What I'm trying to say, Mr Barrowman, is that all of this is highly irregular."

"Irregular, why?"

"Think about it. If the killer really wants to murder every member of your old counselling group, then why would the police risk putting them all under one roof? It's absurd. It goes against every security procedure I've ever encountered. No organisation worth their salt would make such clumsy arrangements. And believe me, with my military knowledge of like operations, I know what I'm talking about. For example, if I was in charge of guarding important people whose lives may well be at risk, I would make sure they were kept miles apart, at secret, heavily guarded locations, not in a remote farmhouse with a solitary squad car outside."

This contingency had never entered my mind. But now it had been pointed out, it did seem strange, ominous even – for surely I was far less exposed in a holding cell at Ilford police station than I was here.

"Did you, erm…talk to the police about this?"

"Of course I did," he said. "And their response was deeply troubling, not to mention suspicious. Watson, the chap heading the murder investigation, made up some story about them being close to a breakthrough, that the main suspect was under strict surveillance. But if that's the case, then surely they'd move in straight away and make an arrest. Four people have been brutally murdered, for pity's sake! The sooner the killer is in police custody, the better."

"But why would the police be so lax?"

"That's the question I've been asking myself ever since they requested that I join you here." He shifted position, straightening in his chair. "Look, Mr Barrowman, I think it's time I told you about a few things I discovered when running a background check on you, things which didn't make any sense at all."

In detail, Bannister told me about a government contact who'd supplied him with medical files, primarily concerning Doctor Rabie's groundbreaking treatment.

"If you know the right people, you can get hold of any information you require. When I looked into Rabie's background, focusing on the work he undertook around the time you were under his care, I found a string of anomalies. There was no official record of him working with your group, despite the fact he makes consistent if unspecified reference to the treatment he oversaw in his academic work. This threw me for a number of reasons. First and foremost, a therapist of his stature wouldn't carry out an eighteen-month experimental treatment programme, and not record his findings. Confused, I checked out the old public building where your meetings took place. And again, there was no record of any group meeting being held there for the duration of your treatment. It's as if everything had been conducted in utmost secrecy, as if it never took place – officially, anyway."

"But we met every week! I swear! Our parents had to sign forms, all kinds of disclaimers, they paid substantial fees. I heard my mother and father talking about it. Surely there must be some official record of all of that."

"No. Nothing. So it got me thinking – maybe not straight away, but later, when Michelle disappeared – about how I'd got involved in all of this, the kinds of things she confided in me regarding her past psychiatric treatment. More and more, I recalled certain conversations we'd had, the way she fed me pieces of information, as if she was leaving a trail, one that would ultimately lead me to looking into Rabie's sessions."

"Why? I don't understand."

"Well, maybe Michelle asked for my help, maybe she befriended me because she wanted me to find out about the past abuse, to discover that she'd been the victim not of a violent partner – who, at the time, I presumed was you, Mr Barrowman – but something much, much darker."

"But that doesn't make sense," I said, trying to follow the logical progression of his theory. "If that really is the case, and four people have been killed, then who's doing the killing?"

"That we can only speculate upon. But perhaps somebody is murdering people to cover up something far worse."

"But what could be worse than taking someone's life?"

"Child abuse, a paedophile ring, a network that goes right up to the corridors of power. Which, conveniently, brings us round to the next piece of information that proved somewhat baffling. When I dug around your employment records, focusing on your time with the local council, I found a letter of recommendation."

I blinked in confusion. I knew nothing about any such letter being written on my behalf.

"It was penned by a prominent barrister, appealing to the local authority to give a troubled yet highly intelligent young man – and I'm certain that was the exact phrase he used – a modest administrative post. He went on to list your good qualities, your high I.Q. and positive response to psychiatric treatment, saying that you came from a hard-working background, that the social services had provided you with accommodation walking distance from the office, and that he would take it as a personal favour if the Area Coordinator could find a suitable job for you to do. Imagine my surprise, when hearing about you going missing, Mr Barrowman, and that your last known whereabouts was at the house of a certain Mrs Forbes-Powers. On hearing the name, alarm bells went off in my head. Checking my notes, I discovered that the barrister who'd written that letter of recommendation was the lady's late husband, Thomas Forbes-Powers."

"Her husband?"

"That's right. So you see: many inexplicable, baffling events have already taken place."

"Well, yes, that goes without saying. And you're not the only to have discovered some unsettling information."

I told him about the letter, the one I sent to Cara all those years ago, and how the women in the dining-room had, quite understandably, in light of the things I'd written, acted with such hostility towards me.

"But couldn't it just have been a case of youthful exuberance, Mr Barrowman? I mean, we all said and did foolish, cringe worthy things when we were teenagers, especially where young ladies were concerned."

"No, no, you don't understand. In the letter, I say some incredibly distasteful things. I—" The door creaked open, we both turned to see Liz poking her head around the jamb.

"Nigel?" she said, squinting up her eyes, as if she wasn't sure if it was really me sitting at the desk in the dim lamplight.

Uncertainly, I got to my feet and walked over to the door. Stepping inside, Liz met me halfway across the room. We hugged each other, but her embrace was lukewarm, almost reluctant, as if she wasn't really sure if she should be wrapping her arms around me like this.

"Are you okay?" I asked. "I've been so worried about you. And I'm so sorry for dragging you into all of this."

"No, no." She lowered her eyes. "It's not your fault some nutcase has gone on a murder spree, is it? I just didn't know what to think when you went missing. I was worried sick, fearing the worst, that you might turn up dead. Then the police dragged me in for questioning, making all kinds of insinuations, making out that you might be involved in the killings somehow."

"I know, I know. Everything is so difficult to explain. I don't know where to begin."

Politely, seeing that we needed some time alone, Bannister excused himself from the room, citing the desperate need for a nice cup of tea. Liz and I sat in the two chairs near the writing desk. Still, our words didn't come easy. It took many a false start and infuriating silence before we finally began to relay information, fill in the blank spaces that defined the last few days.

"That's the thing that don't make no sense," said Liz, "– that bloody wooden box, the one I got from my dad's mate down Portobello, 'cause he's had a stall there ever since I can remember, ever since I was a kiddie, and now he's just up and disappeared."

"Yeah, I couldn't understand that, either. But whoever's been doing all of this must've been following me around, must've known that you and I had become, erm...friendly.

It's the only logical explanation."

"What? And sorta planted the box on the stall?"

"Unlikely as it sounds; it's the only thing that makes any sense."

In as much detail as I dare, I told her about the time I spent in the basement, and how Bannister had found a link between not just the widow's husband but my job at the council.

"Bloody hell! So do you think his wife pushed you down those steps for a reason?"

I hadn't really had time to put it together in my head like that. But now Liz had done so, it seemed more likely than a stranger locking me away, almost at random.

"Look, there's something else I've got to tell you, something you might not want to hear, but something you really need to know." I glanced at the letter open on the desk. "The women staying here, the other members of my old counselling group, have got a serious grudge against me."

I tried to explain about the nature of the letter, the horrible, perverted things I'd committed to paper, even though I had no memory of writing those words, no memory of the events described in those pages.

"Oh, right," she said, nodding slowly, "–that makes sense, then. 'Cause when I arrived and asked where you were, they sort'a exchanged weird looks, they didn't answer for ages, as if they weren't gonna tell me."

I hesitated before saying, "Liz, I know this is a big ask, and I know you haven't known me all that long, and I know there must be all kinds of conflicting things running through your head at the moment, but I'm certain I'm not the person they think I am, I'm certain I never did the things they claim I did. So, for now, it would mean a lot to me if you could just take me as you find me, or found me a week or so back, and not listen if they tell you all kinds of horror stories about me."

A single knock sounded against the door.

"Mr Barrowman." Bannister opened the door a crack.

"The young ladies have just told me that it's twenty minutes until lights out, so if you and Miss Green would like to come up to the communal sleeping quarters now, it would be much appreciated. That way, we can each be allocated a bed."

"All I'm saying," said Cara, standing in the centre of a large room decked out with beds like a dormitory in a hostel, "is that I'm deeply uncomfortable with the idea of sleeping in the same room as someone like him." She jabbed a finger in my direction. "I'm sorry to be so blunt, Nigel, but we all know you of old, and we all know what you're capable of."

I felt like arguing, telling them that they were mistaken, that they'd brainwashed themselves into believing something that simply wasn't true, but Bannister interceded before I could.

"Look, ladies, whatever your former feelings towards Mr Barrowman, we're all in the same boat, and simply have to get on with things as best we can. What I suggest, therefore, is that Mr Barrowman and I share the large bed over there." He pointed across the room. "Due to my military service, I'm a very light sleeper, so you have my personal guarantee that should Mr Barrowman attempt to get up in the night for any other reason than to use the bathroom, he'll have to get past me first. Moreover, there's a constable stationed just down the hallway." He looked at each woman in turn. "Agreed?"

This seemed to go some way to placating them. They nodded out their collective assent, whispered amongst themselves, and started to shuttle to and from the bathroom, before climbing into bed. As Bannister patted my shoulder, as if to reassure me, I looked across the room at Liz, perched on the edge of a camp-bed, head lowered, a distant, thoughtful expression on her face, and I felt, even though only a short period of time had passed, even further away from her than I had in the study earlier.

Chapter Twenty-Nine

At breakfast, it was clear that two distinct factions now existed within the house – them and us. Whether the other women had made a conscious decision to ostracise me, Liz and Bannister from the group was, of course, impossible to say. What was evident, though, was the horrible atmosphere, the tension. As we spooned cereals from bowls to mouths or took slurps of coffee or tea, no one attempted to make any kind of conversation, bar Cara asking Jane to pass her the sugar bowl. Thankfully, before the atmosphere became too poisonous, a chubby, middle-aged detective, a slightly unkempt man, despite wearing a perfectly presentable suit and tie, walked into the kitchen through the back door.

"Morning. Hope you all slept well. For those who don't know" – he looked at me, Liz and Bannister in turn – "I'm Detective Inspector Cattermole. It's my job to make sure that you've all been properly briefed regarding the present situation and have everything that you need."

"Understood," said Banister. "But have there been any new developments? When I left Ilford yesterday, I was told that the main suspect was, and I quote, 'under surveillance'."

The confused looked that broke out over Cattermole's face momentarily betrayed him.

"Well, erm...yes and no," he said, slowly, as if to buy himself some thinking time. "Unfortunately, no arrests have yet to be made, but the noose is definitely tightening, so to speak."

Under the table, Bannister nudged my knee, clearly to indicate how unconvincing he found Cattermole's reply.

"Now," said the policeman, having quickly regained his

composure, "as you've all been made aware, you are being kept here until such a time as we feel it safe for you to return to your homes. I know it's frustrating, and I know how desperate you are to get back to your families, your places of work or study, your everyday lives, but I'm afraid it may be several more days before that's possible."

Bannister couldn't help but go on the offensive.

"If that's the case, Detective Inspector, then I really must voice a few concerns. Firstly, if our lives are in danger, if the killer intends to murder us all, then why are we being kept together, under one roof, instead of at different locations? Secondly, why is there so little security in place? And by that I mean, a single car with two officers guarding the property overnight."

"Appearances can be deceptive," Cattermole said with far more confidence than before. "Let me assure you, teams of highly trained men are patrolling the surrounding woodland, day and night. All entry roads have been cordoned off. In addition, crack marksmen have rifles trained on the house at all times, front and back."

"But if such provisions have been put in place," said Bannister, "it would suggest that you're using us as bait to lure the killer in."

"No, no, not at all," Cattermole replied. "Because of the remote location, how difficult the area is to access, we've used this property in many like situations, without any adverse incidents whatsoever."

Even though Bannister made a few more pointed remarks, questioning the wisdom of the whole operation, Cattermole parried them off with a series of quite reasonable if brusque, somewhat clichéd, stock answers.

"Thank for your time," he said. "If you have any further questions, if there's anything worrying you, if you want to speak to a senior officer regarding the case, please ask the constable on duty, and he'll contact somebody direct."

"You heard what the detective said." Gloria looked, strangely enough, not at us three newcomers, but Cara and

Wendy, perhaps indicating that they were the two women most opposed to interaction. "We're here for the foreseeable future, so why don't we go into the other room and talk things through? Why don't we discuss everything we know about the case, about everything that's happened? Who knows? We might stumble upon something important, something that's been staring us in the face all along."

As we politely waited for the women to exit the room first, Bannister leaned close to me and whispered:

"That Cattermole chappy didn't exactly fill one with confidence, did he, Mr Barrowman? The more I think about this arrangement, the more I don't like it. In my time, I've witnessed countless interrogations, and can tell when someone's lying to me."

"Right." Cara lit a cigarette, wafting smoke away from her face with her free hand. "Like Gloria said, from what we've just been told, it looks like we're going to he holed up here for a long time, well, for the next few days, at the very least. So perhaps it would be best if we talked about everything that's happened." We all murmured in agreement. "And perhaps it would be best if Nigel spoke first. He was, after all, the point of contact, the person the killer singled out."

Nervously, I started to relay every incident, as I had to the police many times before. When I came to the part about the shape I'd randomly doodled on a piece of paper at work, the one Liz recognised as a horned owl, Wendy cried out, her legs buckled, she stumbled forward, and would've collapsed to the floor, had Bannister not leapt to his feet and caught her.

"Wendy!" Cara rushed over and crouched beside her. "What is it?"

But as we all crowded round, it was clear that Wendy wasn't going to be able to answer, that she was in the throes of some kind of fit or seizure.

"Let me through," said Jane, the same doughty, purposeful young woman I remembered from our counselling sessions. "I'm a fully qualified first-aider."

With quick, assured movements, she lowered Wendy down into what I presumed was the recovery position, to ensure that she wouldn't choke or swallow her tongue, supporting her head with a cushion she requested Bannister pull from the armchair he'd so hastily vacated.

"That's it, that's it," Jane spoke soft, reassuring words while gently stroking Wendy's hair and face. Then she turned and addressed us all, "Don't worry. She's going to be just fine. I think it was more of an extreme panic attack than anything else."

"Panic attack?" said Bannister. "Triggered off when Mr Barrowman mentioned the horned owl." He got to his feet. "Did any of you know about the markings cut into the murder victims' bodies? Did any of you know about the Native American fable about the horned owl?"

All shook their heads.

"That's interesting," he said. "But clearly it means something to Miss Lomas here. Yes." He stared into space for a moment. "Why don't we get her a glass or water, or a nice cup of tea, wait until she recovers, and see if we can find out why?"

We all helped Wendy get comfortable, laying her out on the settee, back propped up by cushions, every now and then giving her a sip of water, until she was able to recognise her surroundings, nod her head, and answer simple questions. But as soon as Bannister mentioned the horned owl, her face drained of colour, she looked visibly disturbed, and took to mumbling again.

"The owl, that – that was the signal," she jabbered away, her eyes darting right and left, not so much staring at each one of us, but through us, as if we were invisible to her now.

"Look," said Cara. "This isn't working. She's clearly not up to answering any questions right now. Why don't we let her get some rest?"

Realising this was the sensible thing to do, Bannister and I helped her up the stairs to the communal bedroom, so she could lie down for an hour or two, in hope that that would assist in a full recovery.

When we returned to the front room, the women were deep in discussion.

"The only thing I can think of," said Gloria, acknowledging us with a nod of the head, "when Wendy mumbled something about a signal, was the abortive hypnotherapy sessions we undertook at the beginning of our treatment."

"The what?" I said, shuffling forward a few paces, having no memory whatsoever of being put under hypnosis.

"Don't you remember?" Gloria asked. "At the very first session, Doctor Rabie took us, individually, one at a time, to that back room, what he called his office, but which was really just an old storeroom with a table and a few chairs in it, and tried to put us under hypnosis. But, as it was group therapy, he needed total compliance, and some of us were harder than others to put under hypnosis, to the point of outright defiance, so he decided to forgo that part of the treatment, said it would be self-defeating otherwise."

As time passes, people's memories naturally become a little fuzzy, especially regarding the more minor, insubstantial details of life, but for me to have no recollection of something as unusual, not to mention controversial, as hypnotherapy, something which would undoubtedly have stuck in even the most sieve-like of minds, was impossible for me to accept.

"Wait just a minute. We were never hypnotised. Our therapy consisted of what most modern therapists would now call organic, primal treatment. Once we'd got over the initial unease, once we were more comfortable, we were instructed to sit on the floor facing each other, and talk about our problems. Whenever something especially disturbing arose, Doctor Rabie would encourage us to shout, to scream into each others faces, until we'd neutralised the problem, defusing the mind bomb, as he called it. To suggest that we—"

"No, no." Cara wagged a finger in the air, "I really am going to have to stop you there, Nigel. At the first session, after we had to go through that excruciating procession of standing up, saying our names, and telling each other a little bit about ourselves, Doctor Rabie outlined the stages of our treatment, the first part of which would involve hypnotherapy, a new way to help us subconsciously confront our problems. Why would any of us make something like that up?"

"I have no idea. Like I have no idea why you harbour such antipathy towards me, why you see me as someone I'm so obviously not."

What had started out as a sensible discussion, an attempt to exchange useful information regarding the murders, denigrated into a full-blown argument, with Cara and Gloria in particular insisting that we were all, at some stage, put under hypnosis.

"This is getting us nowhere." Cara clicked her tongue. "Why don't we take a break, go for a walk in the garden, get some air? Then, after lunch, maybe Wendy will feel up to talking to us."

Still riled, still arguing with them in my head, conjuring belated yet compelling counterarguments, I was surprised to feel a tap on my shoulder, and hear Jane's whispered voice.

"Nigel." She drew me back into the room as the others passed through to the kitchen. "Can I have a quick word?"

"Of course," I said, looking on as she pushed the door to. "What is it?"

She handed me a slim wallet file.

"Here, take this. Inside are the surviving parts of my journal, the one I was writing at the time of our treatment with Doctor Rabie. I'd like you to read it. I'd like to know what you make of it. Because I – I don't think the other girls have treated you very fairly."

"How do you mean?"

"That I don't remember you in the same way they do. To the best of my memory – and believe me, there's not a day goes by when I don't question myself, and what really happened back then – until Cara received that letter, the one she showed you last night, you were all the things you claimed to be: quiet, shy, withdrawn, the most distant and disturbed member of the group, someone who rarely if ever contributed, someone who verged upon tears if ever asked to stand up and speak."

"Then why didn't you say something last night?"

"Because nobody liked you, Nigel. Because you did make us feel incredibly uncomfortable, just not in the way the girls' said. But because you were so vulnerable, on edge, like you might do something silly, hurt yourself, maybe take your own life, like a mirror image of the very worst, most desperate versions of ourselves imaginable. And we didn't want to see that every week. It was too close to home."

An awkward, prickly silence.

"But, please," she said, touching my hand, the one holding the file, "read what's inside. To be honest, I have no recollection of writing any of it, but, seen through another set of eyes, it might make some kind of sense."

Chapter Thirty

To describe what I found inside Jane's file is a difficult task. The neat, handwritten, perfectly legible sheets of paper didn't really constitute a linear journal or diary, more a stream of consciousness, fractured reminisces, notes, reflections, but things which nevertheless felt vaguely familiar to me. In the opening pages, for example, she had written what is probably best described as a rudimentary self-critique, examining her condition in relation to an everyday situation, trying to work out why she had reacted in a certain way, when offering to wash up following a family meal. It was something Jane often did, so she relayed, just to help out, to play the role of a normal seventeen-year-old girl. But, in trying to assist, her mother and father cleared some of the plates from the table and brought them through to the kitchen, placing them on the work surface near the sink. This annoyed Jane, because the kitchen was quite small and cramped, and she knew it would be quicker and easier if her parents simply let her clear the plates and wash them herself. In her head, therefore, that inexplicable rage, the likes of which anyone who's suffered from mental problems, who's struggled to operate in normal everyday situations, is so sadly familiar with, began to rise.

As if wanting to exacerbate things, to make herself angrier, even more unreasonable, Jane started to notice all kinds of 'vexing concomitants'. Firstly, that her mother's used cutlery had slid into the middle of the plate, and was now marooned in a pool of thick leftover gravy, which meant that when Jane picked them up to wash them (she had a strict routine: cutlery first, then plates, then pots and pans), she'd get residual gravy stains on her fingers, she'd have to literally wade through someone's dirty plate – and such thoughtlessness seemed completely unacceptable, almost akin to a deliberate insult.

As this festered, her father reached over her at the sink, to fill a glass with water (he was Type 2 diabetic and had to take several pills directly after each meal). But the way in which he did this, brusquely, without so much as saying excuse me, like his daughter was no more than a skivvy, or worse, invisible, infuriated Jane all over again. To the extent that she had to turn away, take a breath, squeeze her eyes shut, count to ten – all the flimsy fail-safes counsellors had drummed into her whenever she felt she was about to lose control. Then her mother belched loudly, laughed, and excused herself. And it seemed to Jane, flustered by the crush of bodies, the way in which her parents were still crowding around her, when all she wanted to do was the 'fucking washing up', that her mother belched at exactly the same time each day, following each meal, and this sense of things repeating themselves, of being trapped, where each day was exactly the same as the one that had preceded it, sent her over the edge. Screaming, telling her parents to 'fuck off, will you, get away from me', she picked up a plate and smashed it on the floor. In the chaotic, confused moments that followed, she tried to apologise, sweep up the broken plate, to explain why she'd lost control, that if they'd only let her get on with the washing up in peace, then none of this would have happened. But, of course, that was impossible now. In reacting in the way she did, she had no recourse to reasonable explanation – she was the bad guy, the nutcase who couldn't control her temper.

And this incident, although minor, trivial, stupid in many ways, seemed indicative of everything else in Jane's life. So much so she felt like killing herself, taking a knife and slashing her wrists again, just so she could leave a note to her parents, blaming them for her death, saying if only her mother hadn't left her cutlery in a pool of gravy then none of this would've happened. 'That's how insignificant my life experience really is'.

On the next page, Jane wrote about a session with Doctor Rabie, but in a quite unorthodox way, like a journalist taking rapid-fire notes at a sporting event:

He knows more than he's letting on, we are not being treated for mental illness, our welfare is of no importance to him or his superiors, we are being slowly brainwashed (this, in fact, she crossed out, replacing it with: we are slowly having our memories erased), the shouting and screaming conceals present events not those locked away in our past, when he asks us to let go of a troubling thought, he is asking us to forgot, to absolve him of blame, he knows the medication is unsuitable yet he increases the dosage, he knows which ones of us are most vulnerable yet presses us hardest of all, he will undoubtedly meet a bloody end.

A little further on:

Michelle is the key. During each session, I watch her closely, analysing her movements, expressions, the way her face sometimes betrays her emotions, mentally recording everything she says and does. In turn, I notice the way Doctor Rabie always treats her with extreme deference. In circumstances where he might be forceful and demanding of others, pushing us to answer a particularly uncomfortable question, he will let Michelle off, praising her for efforts she didn't really make. Important point: with everyone else, he is very tactile, a skilful exponent of touch, utilising the reassuring pat on the back or arm around the shoulder, a warm handshake (always making eye contact), to put us at ease. But with Michelle he refrains from all kind of bodily contact, as if there is an invisible exclusion zone encircling her, as if she is too precious too touch. This only reaffirms my theory. If Michelle is the key, then she must've been the first one to be taken against her will. There's a signal, if only I could remember the signal.

Then she backtracked and wrote:

Everybody's signal is different, so I have no way of breaking each individual code. If only I could remember mine, I might be able to fool him, act as if I'm under his spell, and then learn all his secrets.

Towards the end, I found several handwritten sheets, different in tone to the preceding pages, as if she'd copied passages direct from a textbook.

Hypnotherapy alters the patient's subconscious mind.

The hypnotised patient is far more open and suggestible.

Victorian physicians used hypnosis to cure hysteria, whereas contemporary hypnosis is used to treat a far broader range of emotional and psychological disorders.

This was, to a certain extent, the theory behind electrical shock treatments undertaken in the United States during the later 1950s and early 60s, whereby, for instance, if an adolescent boy displayed homosexual tendencies, shock treatment to the part of the brain controlling sexual desire, attraction, would hopefully remove these tendencies altogether.

In the mid 1980s Doctor Lawrence Rabie, a renowned psychotherapist, undertook what he himself described as a groundbreaking hypnotherapeutic research, whereby he attempted to reverse the standard processes by bombarding a patient's hypnotised subconscious mind with behavioural stimuli, which could then be aroused in the conscious mind – i.e. making patients adopt certain modes of behaviour, to act and think in a prescribed manner. This was usually triggered off by a key word, or signal of some kind, like clapping the hands or a shrill whistle. If successful, Rabie would then, in effect, be able to control his patients' thoughts and actions in everyday life.

Chapter Thirty-One

"Where have you been hiding, Mr Barrowman?" Bannister met me in the hallway, a moment after I'd slipped out of the study and closed the door. "Miss Green has been looking for you."

I told him about Jane and the somewhat cryptic contents of the file I'd just spent the last hour or so reading.

"So, if Miss Lines makes concrete reference to hypnotherapy in her journal, that would give my theory even more credence."

"Theory? What theory?"

Bannister looked right and left, as if fearful of being overheard.

"Come with me." He gestured to the stairs. "I know you're probably eager to speak to Miss Green, but let's lock ourselves away in the bathroom for fifteen or twenty minutes, let's go over all the new information, and assess exactly where it leaves us."

"Before you tell me about the specific contents of the file," said Bannister, "I must make you aware of my recent activities, outside, while reconnoitring the area. Surprisingly, the extent of garden into which we are allowed to wander is quite large, affording a dramatic view over the undulating countryside, fields and hills. Having looked the area up and down, I'm convinced that there are no guards or marksmen in the woodland surrounding the farmhouse. If there were, they would be positioned at certain strategic vantage points, obvious to anyone with military training. But on a comprehensive survey, there was no sign of a military presence whatsoever. More worrying, though, it looks like the main road from the dirt-track is still fully operational. Through the trees, one can see and hear all kinds of vehicles – cars, vans, tractors and suchlike – none of which appear to slow down at any checkpoint or cordon."

"But why would Cattermole lie to us like that? Surely you don't think they've rounded us up here simply to hold us prisoner, or – or kill us and dispose of our bodies in the most expedient way possible, do you?"

Bannister's brief silence told me that that was exactly his current train of thought.

"I never like to make a judgment without access to all relevant information. But that doesn't mask the fact that we're sitting ducks. Now, tell me about this file, the one Miss Lines requested that you read."

The contents still fresh in my mind, I went through each individual section of the journal, making special reference to the insightful observations she had made about Rabie, Michelle, and the notes she appeared to have copied from a hypnotherapy textbook.

"That's very interesting, Mr Barrowman, very interesting indeed. If you were all subject to effective hypnotherapy, it would account for you all having different memories of what took place during the counselling sessions. Perhaps Doctor Rabie did have control of your subconscious, perhaps he made you write that letter to Miss Clarke, perhaps we really are dealing with a plot of some kind, a cover-up, the secret of which lies deep in the recesses of your mind."

As much as I hated to admit it, Bannister's theory was the most plausible I'd yet to hear.

"You know, all of this brings to mind a covert operation I was involved in, one that had serious ramifications for the entire Middle East peace process. Via a network of underground informants, my team had infiltrated a group of local militia, intent on overthrowing a political figure I better not mention by name. Assassination was our ultimate objective. But getting close to this despot wasn't going to be easy. After months of deliberation, where the situation on the ground was only worsening, we came to a drastic decision. On the inside, we had an operative, a member of the domestic staff who interacted with our target on a daily basis. Only we weren't sure if we could trust him implicitly, certainly not to carry out what would in effect be a suicide mission."

"What happened?"

"Well, my commanding officer was a very resourceful individual. Thinking out of the box, as if were, he flew a renowned hypnotherapist in from Israel, a man who, again, it's probably best if I don't mention by name. The plan was to hypnotise our inside man, to delve deep into his subconscious mind, planting a hidden signal, to murder our target at a prearranged time. All of which was to be triggered off by a keyword. Before we undertook the operation, we, of course, had to carry out a few experiments, to see if the hypnosis was indeed effective, for if the operation failed, the target would know that the security services were plotting his assassination, and would disappear deeper underground, so deep we would probably never get the opportunity to kill him again.

"The results of the hypnosis, however, were as astounding as they were comical. To showcase his mastery of the field, the hypnotherapist convinced the subject that he was a dog, and had him down on all fours, chasing after his own tail. All of which proved, or so we thought at the time, that the operation, radical as it was, had a very high chance of success.

"That day, everything went to plan. Our operative entered the heavily armed complex as normal, and set about his daily work duties. At the appointed hour, he was called to his master's chamber to serve refreshments. From reconnaissance reports, we knew he had a serious weakness for, of all things, Coca-Cola, and, accordingly, that was our key word, our signal, the trigger. Only–"

"Only what?"

"Only when the target said the keyword, our operative didn't act in the way we had expected. No. He grabbed a sabre from a guard, cried God is great, and slit his own throat in front of his master."

"What? Why?"

"Because the human mind is a very complex thing, Mr Barrowman. Not once during our trial runs did our man display any resistance. But, deep inside, his allegiance to his leader, his country, his family, his religion was far too great."

"So there was a part of his brain which, in effect, overrode the subconscious instructions."

"Exactly. I couldn't have put it better myself. And when he heard the words Coca-Cola, he reacted in the only honourable way he knew – killing himself not his spiritual leader." Bannister shook his head. "No. Not even medical specialists should tinker with a man's mind like that. There can only be dire long-term consequences."

We lapsed into silence.

"Mr Bannister," I then asked, struck by something from what felt like another lifetime ago now, "can I ask you a personal question?"

"Of course you can."

"Your, erm…ex-wife, did she ever attack you with a weapon, a knife or…?"

Uncharacteristically, Bannister took a long time before answering.

"Let's just say she left her mark on me forever more, Mr Barrowman, and leave it at that." He checked his wristwatch. "Come on. Best we go downstairs. Best we tell the others everything we now know."

Chapter Thirty-Two

"So let me get this straight," said Cara, pacing the front room, "you expect us to believe that we're being held here as prisoners. And that, in all likelihood, the police, on orders from an unknown authority, people of power and influence, who may have had some sick twisted interest in us when we were younger, have created this situation, to, in effect, gag us, to stop us from finding out the truth."

"I make such an assertion," said Bannister, "on the evidence as I interpret it. And if, for instance, Miss Rouse wrote a wholly fictitious set of diaries, a wholly fictitious set of correspondence with Mr Barrowman – and I think at this stage, we all agree that that is more than just a possibility – then it's likely that, under hypnotherapy, he, and I mean Mr Barrowman, composed the letter to Miss Clarke."

"To provide an alibi," said Jane, "to plant seeds of doubt, you mean, to give them a—"

"An alibi for what, though?" cried Gloria, her patience clearly stretched. "You're talking in riddles. You're—"

"For whatever happened to us in those group sessions," I interrupted. "Because, let's face it, if we all have completely different memories of a collective experience then someone, somewhere along the line, must've tampered with our minds." I turned to Wendy. "Before you passed out earlier, you said something about the horned owl being the signal. Can you remember saying that? And, if so, what did you mean?"

Wendy took a few short, shallow breaths and lowered her eyes.

"Well, after our sessions with Doctor Rabie stopped, I – I suffered from terrible nightmares. It always started with the owl, a sharp hooting noise, incredibly loud, right outside my bedroom window. When I got out of bed and pulled back the curtains I'd see these terrifying eyes, glowing yellow, staring back at me. And as I cowered, turned and tried to run away, that's when they grabbed hold of me."

"They?" several of us said at once.

"Yes. The men, the ones who wanted to hurt us."

This shook us all to silence.

"Look," said Bannister. "What if Miss Lomas' nightmare was not merely a frightening dream, but a subconscious memory, a memory of what really happened to you during your counselling sessions?"

"But that's absurd," said Cara, stubbing out another cigarette, "like a conspiracy theory."

"And even if there is some truth to it," said Gloria, "what are we supposed to do now? If the police are involved, complicit in the wrongdoing, maybe even guilty of murdering our friends, who do we turn to?"

"Exactly!" said Bannister. "There are no phone lines here. I've checked. Apparently, the place is often used as a writers' retreat, contact with the outside world, therefore, is seen as an unnecessary and unwelcome distraction. Those of you who have mobile phones have had them confiscated, for, so the police said, fear of the murderer tracing your signal."

"We know all this," said Cara. "Still you haven't told us what we're going to do."

"That's because I'm not sure," said Bannister, "– not yet. In the twenty-odd hours since I've been here, I've felt increasingly uncomfortable about the whole situation. Mainly because we're so vulnerable, because we have so few options available to us. For instance, if you find my theory so hard to believe, then go outside and talk to the constables on duty, demand to speak to a senior officer, confront the situation head on. Or, alternatively, we could wait until the early hours of the morning, sneak out of the house, get up onto the motorway and hail down a car, head into London, contact the press, try to bring as much attention to ourselves as we possibly can."

"You mean all of us?" said Gloria, "– on foot, in pitch darkness, across muddy fields and all sorts."

"Couldn't you go alone?" said Jane. "Sneak off and call for help?" A reasonable enough suggestion, or so I thought at the time, but Bannister shook his head.

"If I went alone, and something happened to the rest of you while I was gone, it would defeat the object of trying to get out of here safely. No? What I propose, therefore, to wrong-foot the police, to conceal our true concerns, is a reconnaissance mission. Tomorrow, after breakfast, when the police are least expecting a disturbance, I will sneak out of the garden, enter the adjoining woodland, and search for the nearest property, maybe even a vehicle, one large enough to accommodate us all, something I could potentially commandeer to effect an escape. Then, if and when the time comes, we'll, at the very least, have a plan of action in place." He looked at us all in turn. "Agreed?"

Chapter Thirty-Three

"Sorry about my disappearing act," I said to Liz as we sat down in the study. "Only I thought it best to have a look at Jane's journal straight away. And I'm glad I did. At least not everyone here remembers me as such a horrible bastard."

"I know, and I'm glad, too. Jesus, that Cara has certainly got it in for you. Earlier, in the garden, she took me aside, asked all kinds of questions – whether you'd ever hit me or asked me to do anything I didn't wanna do, you know, sexually. She warned me off you, told me a couple of horror stories about you and that Jeffrey Fuller fella."

"About me and Jeffrey? What kinds of stories?"

In light of everything, I shouldn't have asked. Whatever Cara had to say about me could only be monstrous, a gross misrepresentation.

"'Bout the time you and him spiked a dog's water bowl with a sedative."

Apparently, one afternoon, Jeffrey and I abducted a local dog, a quite rare breed, although Cara wasn't quite sure what it was, mashed the sedative up in its food, and dragged it down the park, near the swings where some much younger children were playing – in the main, ten-year-old girls. Calling them over, we rolled the dog onto its back, exposing its genitalia, Jeffrey working its penis back and forth, until it ejaculated, horrifying everyone present.

"She said that the police got involved, said that you made Jeffrey take the blame, that he had to spend a night in the cells, that it really messed his head up, that he was never the same again."

Of all the things Cara could've said, acts of borderline bestiality were probably the last I expected. Still, there was something in what Liz had just relayed that got me thinking.

"That's strange. In our group therapy sessions, I remember Jeffrey saying something about being locked up and drugged, about coming round, being naked and bound, surrounded by men in leather masks. But he said it in such a way I thought it was just another one of his filthy fantasies."

"Did he do that a lot, then?"

"Yeah, yeah he did," I said, struck by something else, a flood of Jeffrey Fuller inspired recollections. Because nearly everything he said back then revolved around sexual abuse, usually a dramatic, detailed rape scene. Maybe, like the rest of us, with the letters and diaries, he wasn't just regurgitating his most sordid sexual fantasies to shock and disturb, but wrestling with his own subconscious mind, reliving abuse he may've suffered at another's hands.

"What is it?"

"Oh, nothing," I replied, not wanting to burden her with such dark, uncomfortable conjecture. "I was just thinking about—"

"Look, Nigel, I wanted to have a chat with you alone, 'cause I'm not sure if us being us is a very good idea anymore."

"What? Why? Because of everything that's happened. Because of the murders and what the others said and—"

"It's not just about the murders, the police and everything. And I know you're not the kind of person those stuck-up muppets upstairs are trying to make out you are. Only I don't know if there's much of a future for us, you know. I just wanna simple, hassle-free relationship. I just wanna be normal. I've been through too much in the past. I ain't got the strength to go through it again. I think, maybe, when it comes down to it, we're both too damaged to make a serious go of things."

"But I thought we were good together, that we brought the best out in each other."

"So did I. But relationships are hard enough without all this baggage. I wanna do my voluntary work at The Samaritans, to help as many people as I can, hopefully become a proper qualified social worker or counsellor or something one day. But when I get home of a night, I just wanna cuddle up on the sofa in front of *Eastenders*, drink a can of cider, order a kebab, and I don't think that would ever be enough for you."

Inevitably, I tried to talk Liz round, telling her not to make any hasty decisions, that I understood exactly how she felt, that maybe it would be best if we took a break from each other, just until the police apprehended the murderer, then, perhaps, we could start again.

"Let's just leave it, hey?" She got to her feet, leaned over and planted a soft kiss to my cheek. "Let's just concentrate on getting out of here in one piece." She straightened and walked towards the door, saying over her shoulder, "I'll see you in the morning, yeah?"

After she'd left me alone, there was an ominous, crystallised stillness to the room, the house, the world and everything in it. I don't know what it was – sadness, regret, an anti-climax – as if I'd been a valiant hero on a mystical quest to win Liz's hand, and now I didn't have that to strive for, all my efforts had been in vain, that it didn't matter if we ever found out the truth now, if Bannister was right or wrong about the police, whether the killer struck again, if we were all murdered in our sleep, our bodies buried in the surrounding woodland, because, after all this was over, I'd go straight back to my own boring, sad, lonely life, to complete and utter isolation.

I was awoken by a loud, ghostly hooting noise, right outside the study door. I sat up on the settee, blinked my eyes, rubbed my face, and then pinched my forearm really hard, twisting the skin around and around, just to make sure I wasn't dreaming. But I wasn't. Another hoot-hoot was followed by the sound of hurried footsteps bounding up the stairs.

I rushed out of the study, dashing down the hallway.

What happened next happened so quickly, I didn't have time to react, to shout out and warn the others. For no sooner had I reached the foot of the stairs, than two hulking men wearing (and even now, I have grave doubts about what I actually saw) feathered headdresses, just like the Native Americans from the horned owl fable, came running down the last few steps. When they saw me they lashed out, kicking and beating me time and again, knocking me to the stone floor, stamping all over my prostrate body.

After that, all I was aware of were fragmented images, sounds, smells – most of all, flickering orange flames and thick billowing smoke. So thick, I started to cough, choke, until I regained something close to full consciousness. From upstairs came screaming, the crackling sound of fire licking wood, padding feet on floorboards. Blindly I groped for the wall, wiping blood from my face and wafting smoke from my eyes. Hauling myself up to my feet, I made it halfway up the stairs, meeting Bannister through a thick curtain of smoke, carrying a woman in his arms.

"Mr Barrowman!" He handed me Jane, unconscious, unmoving. "Quickly, take her outside. I'll go up for another one. If we act fast, we'll get everybody out."

Somehow I managed to take hold of her without toppling backwards down the stairs, descend the remaining steps, pull open the front door, run outside, and place her on the shingled drive. But it was too late. Jane wasn't breathing; she was dead.

I looked up.

There was no police car parked outside, no officers sitting in the front seat.

I raced back into the house, the smoke so thick now, the flames throwing off such intense heat, it almost forced me straight back out of the door. Pulling my jumper up over my nose, I inched over towards the foot of the stairs, almost colliding with Bannister as he bounded down the last few steps, another body in his arms.

"Here." He handed me the unconscious woman – it was Liz. "Mr Barrowman," he shouted right into my ear, "the fire's getting out of control, but I'll give it one last go; I'll take a chance, smash some windows. See if we can't jump out to safety."

Determined to get Liz out of the house, I turned and ran back through the front door, crouching and laying her down on the drive next to Jane.

"Liz, Liz," I cried, lightly slapping her face, checking for a pulse in her neck. "Please be all right. Please be all right. Liz! Liz!"

Suddenly she opened her eyes, and coughed so violently, I was sure she was going to be sick.

"Don't – Don't worry 'bout me," she murmured. "Go help the others."

As I turned to run back into the house, someone struck me across the back of the head, once again knocking me senseless. The last thing I heard was more screaming; the last thing I saw was a horrible smear of flickering orange flame across my fading peripheral vision. Then everything went black...

Chapter Thirty-Four

The first person I saw when I woke up in a private hospital room was Gideon Forbes-Powers.

"Relax, relax," he said, on hearing me stir. "You've been through a terrible ordeal." He got to his feet, smiled concernedly, and softly patted my shoulder. As he straightened, I noticed the empty sleeve where his left arm had previously been. "Don't overexert yourself."

"Liz, Liz," I tried to say, but my throat was so sore, so tender, the words were probably no more than a croaking jumble of insensible nonsense.

Regardless, Gideon must've understood what I meant. His eyes watery and troubled, he shook his head.

"I'm so sorry, Nigel, but you were the only survivor. Everyone else perished in the blaze, most from smoke inhalation. It was a terrible accident."

The word accident jarred with me to the point where I wanted to leap from the bed, to shout out, to tell him it was anything but an accident, that all those people – Liz, Bannister, everyone – had been murdered. But I felt far too weak to move, break down and cry, too confused to assemble any kind of considered emotional response.

As I struggled to hold myself together, the door swung open and in walked a sprightly, white-coated Indian doctor.

"Ah, Mr Barrowman, you've finally woken up, then." He picked up a chart from the foot of the bed. "You're lucky to be alive. If you hadn't tripped and fallen outside and banged your head like that, you would've no doubt suffered the same fate as the others, including the valorous former soldier, the man to be awarded a posthumous bravery award for his actions, even though they were sadly in vain."

At this point, I decided to play dumb, to feign amnesia, to

make out I had no recollection of what took place at the farmhouse. Even then, in the first few minutes of proper consciousness, I was fully aware of the inevitable, potentially dangerous police questioning that awaited me. If I claimed not to remember anything, it might buy me some breathing space, it might even help to save my life.

"What happened?" I asked, touching the thick bandage bounding my head.

Taking it in turns, the doctor (a Doctor Rashid) and Gideon helped fill the phantom gaps in my memory.

"Apparently,' said Gideon, "one of the women in the house was a heavy smoker. By all accounts, she lit up in the communal bedroom in the early hours of the morning, and must've nodded straight back off to sleep again, dropping the cigarette and starting the blaze. Bloody ridiculous – and so, so avoidable. By the time you and that Bannister chap awoke, it was already too late; the room was engulfed in smoke."

"But what about the policemen guarding the house? Surely they would've been alerted by the blaze. Surely they should've helped tackle the flames."

"Tragically," said Rashid, "the two young officers on duty that night had dropped off to sleep, too. Only when you dashed out of the house with the first body did they awaken and offer any assistance." He clicked his tongue. "With the bedroom being at the back of the property, they simply weren't aware of the fire, they simply didn't see the flames."

Later that day, I received the expected police visit. Two senior, plain-clothed officials (and I call them officials because they told me they were from the Internal Affairs Division), a Dowd and Montgomery, entered the room.

"We're so glad that you're feeling better now, Mr Barrowman," said Dowd. "But, as I'm sure you appreciate, in the aftermath of the incident, we're still trying to piece together exactly what happened. Anything you can tell us about the night in question would, therefore, be greatly appreciated."

I told him I didn't remember anything with any clarity, that it was all a blur, that all that remained in my memory were fragments, like speaking to Liz after I carried her outside. Here, I perhaps betrayed myself slightly, so keen was I to learn exactly what had happened to her, because when I last saw her, she was conscious, lucid, very much alive.

"As she was in the ambulance on the way to the hospital," said Montgomery, the bulkier and more forthcoming of the two men. "Unfortunately, smoke inhalation can creep up on you, can be a silent killer. This proved to be the case with Miss Green and Mr Bannister. By the time she'd been transferred to a hospital bed, she experienced serious breathing difficulties, and despite the doctors and nurses best efforts they couldn't revive her."

I slowly nodded, a vivid image of the men who started the fire, the men in feathered headdresses flashing before my eyes.

"There will, of course, be a full inquiry," said Dowd. "Lessons will have to be learned, especially from a logistical point of view, keeping a number of witnesses, those at risk under one roof, instead of at separate locations."

It was then, as he repeated Bannister's words from the night before the fire, almost verbatim, that I wondered if there had been some sort of wire tap in the farmhouse, that the police had been listening in to us at all times, and that's why they chose to strike right away, that's why they set fire to the house.

"And, erm…what about the murder investigation?" I asked, hoping to both divert my own thoughts and further wrong-foot the officers. "Have there been any arrests? Has Michelle Rouse or her parents been found yet?"

Both men shifted a little uncomfortably.

"You don't know?" said Dowd. "Of course you don't, how could you, being holed up here in the hospital? Yesterday, the bodies of Mr and Mrs Rouse were found in a car, clear suicide, exhaust pipe fumes funnelled into the vehicle via rubber tubing. There was no note, either at the scene or at the deceased couples' home. We can only assume, therefore, that their daughter's lurid allegations had sent them over the edge."

"So you found the diaries, then?"

"No, no," said Montgomery. "We're basing our assumptions on the testimony of both yourself and Mr Bannister, and, of course, the missing woman's medical records."

Chapter Thirty-Five

In the week that followed, while I was still officially recuperating, Gideon visited me twice a day, often staying well beyond official visiting hours. He was so polite and attentive, offering to get me anything I needed, that I had difficulty working out how I felt about him and everything that happened in the basement. Very much in fear of my life, not to mention traumatised by the fire, it didn't feel like I had any friends to turn to, anyone I could trust. Gideon, therefore, became a central figure in my life, a connection with the outside world, a confidant, someone I could rely on.

At my request, he gathered all the newspaper reports of the fire: *Tragedy at Police Safe House, Heroic Ex-Serviceman Dies in Attempt to Save Others, Police to Reassess Procedures Following Fire Deaths* were the general tone of the headlines, although the accompanying articles were almost completely bereft of specific details regarding how the blaze had started, why the police had chosen to house key witnesses in a multiple murder investigation under one roof, and why there wasn't a sufficient police presence guarding the property.

Despite all this, I still had doubts about Gideon, his motivations, not to mention many questions that I wanted to ask about his family, any knowledge he might have of his father's part in securing me employment at the council.

"Gideon," I said towards the end of the week, "can I ask you something? What are you doing here? Why are you being so kind, acting like my next of kin?"

"Well, I, erm…hold myself somewhat responsible for your predicament, old chap. What, with Mater locking you away like that. Unforgivable. I just want to try and make amends." He bit into his bottom lip. "And – And I didn't want to mention this straight away. I didn't want to upset you. But Mater passed away the day after you absconded from the basement. So I've been at a bit of a loose end, a bit lost, after coming out of the hospital myself, not really knowing which way to turn. In many respects, visiting you has helped take my mind off things, the will, funeral arrangements and suchlike."

It felt polite to offer my condolences, but I could only muster a slight nod of the head, a flicker of forced sympathy breaking out across my face.

"Secondly, and this really is the most incredible and unexpected bit of news, but I've been offered a publishing contract for *The Magister's Analects*, a quite amazingly lucrative one at that." He glanced across at me, as if to gauge my reaction. "Only proviso is that I make a few changes to the manuscript following what the publisher called an 'extensive creative edit'. And as you're the only other person in the world who's read a little of the book, I'd like to make you an offer. How about coming on-board, and working with me as an assistant editor?"

"An assistant editor?"

"I know it's a big decision, Nigel, a big commitment. So why don't I let you sleep on it. Tomorrow, I can bring in a copy of the contract for you to look at, maybe even some of the editor's notes on the manuscript, areas that could be tightened and revised, as it were. Only remember, the financial rewards, if the book was to become a success, would be huge."

Next day I declined the offer, having never been particularly enamoured of the subject-matter or tone of the writing.

"So you're saying no, then?" he asked, pacing up and down the room. "You don't want to get involved?"

I tried to explain my decision as soberly as possible, citing my current state of mind (I had been suffering from genuinely terrible nightmares about the fire), my fears for my own future, my job at the council, my flat, neither of which appeared straightforward.

"But you owe me," he cried, waving his empty sleeve around. "If it wasn't for you, I wouldn't be a bloody cripple. I'd have two perfectly good functioning arms."

In a petulant display, he went through the entire gamut of negative emotions – anger, disbelief, spite, outrage.

"Well, I didn't want to tell you this, Nigel, but you've been evicted from your flat, and your contract of employment has been terminated with immediate effect. Unless you come back to the house and work with me, you really don't have anywhere else to go."

I wasn't sure if this was correct, if I could trust him, but it didn't concern me unduly. I'd had so much contact with social services over the years, I knew there was no way I would be without some kind of roof over my head, be it a halfway house or a room in private lodgings, however grotty or unappealing.

And this I told him.

"I wouldn't be so sure," he said, with an ominous edge to his voice. "But I really do need your help. Therefore, I'm prepared to put all my cards on the table."

"All your cards on the table?" I repeated, familiar with the expression, but unsure how it applied to this particular situation. "How do you mean?"

"I mean, that if you help edit the book, I will tell you the truth about your counselling sessions with Doctor Rabie, the whole story, everything you've been struggling to remember all these years."

Chapter Thirty-Six

"I know you've only just come out of the hospital," said Watson from across the interview room table, like a memory of a past event that had only ever taken place in my head, "but some very serious allegations have been made against you. So let's go over things one more time. On the morning in question, you escaped from Mrs Forbes-Powers' house and ran down the street. A car pulled over to the side of the road. Inside was Mr Bannister, the so-called private detective, who just so happened to be passing. He drove you to see Mr and Mrs Rouse, who showed you diaries written by their missing daughter, accusing them of sexual abuse. All three of whom, the parents and Bannister, are now deceased."

"Granted," I said, struggling to maintain my composure. "But Bannister is the same man who recently received a posthumous bravery award, a man who sacrificed his life in an attempt to save many others, a man who made a signed statement attesting to the validity of a great deal of my story. Surely that still holds some weight with you?"

Watson made a vague, pouty, non-committal face.

"Of course it does. But that doesn't discount the fact that you've been identified as the man who ran down an elderly woman, leaving her for dead."

"But that woman has a history of throwing herself in front of vehicles. Check her background, if you don't believe me. Call the bus service or – or the local supermarkets, for that matter. She goes around trying to feign injury in the hope of getting compensation."

"But, Mr Barrowman, this lady was in intensive care for nearly three weeks, she's broken several vertebrae, a leg, an ankle, she may never walk again. Whatever her past, she was struck by a speeding car that you may or may not have been driving. So why not admit to being behind the wheel? The fact you've been involved in a stressful murder investigation will no doubt be a mitigating factor in your defence."

"But that's not how it happened."

But Kendrick and Watson seemed determined to get me to admit to something I hadn't done, telling me how bad it would appear in court if I tried to shift the blame onto Bannister, a recently deceased hero. In the end, in desperation, after what must've have been two or three hours of questioning, I told them that I wanted to see my legal representative.

"I can't lie to you." Price paced up and down the interview room. "Things don't look very promising."

What he reeled off next, I could barely keep up with: witness statements, positive identification, irrefutable claims, an attempted murder charge, my past medical records, erratic behaviour, and potential incarceration at a mental facility.

Only when he said, "It could, however, take three years before your case is up for official review," did I realise the full seriousness of my situation.

"Three years!"

In all, I spent two additional nights in custody, sleeping in the same ugly holding cell as before, and endured hours of additional questioning before I was moved to a high security psychiatric unit. Once in a grim, sparsely furnished private room, my empty future opened up before me. It felt as if I'd come full circle, back to when I started to have mental health problems as a teenager.

The night before the interim hearing, which I was told I wouldn't have to attend in person, I was awoken by a soft rustling sound. As I hauled myself up into a sitting position, I saw that someone had slid a large envelope under the door. Looking right and left, for what or whom I couldn't have said – the room was empty – I crept out of bed, picked up the letter, and went and sat at the desk in the far corner of the room. From the light that came from the window, product of a quite staggeringly bright full moon, I saw that the envelope had been marked for my attention. *F.A.O. Nigel Barrowman* read the top line of the label, printed in an elegant font: Cambria, I think. Carefully, I unsealed the envelope and pulled out the contents, a photograph, enlarged, of someone's wrist, a tattoo of a horned owl scraped across the skin. I gasped, nearly toppled out of the chair, because the wrist clearly belonged to Michelle. There was a distinctive brown birthmark and a freckle near the base of the owl, something impossible to superimpose or photo-shop to anywhere close to this degree.

I turned the envelope over. *YOU WILL DIE A HORRIBLE DEATH* had been printed on the back in neat capital letters.

Chapter Thirty-Seven

On waking, I didn't know where I was; I didn't know what was happening. Overnight the room had changed completely. Now it resembled a strange amalgamation of the holding cell in Ilford, and my bedroom at the flat. And by that I mean, the furniture: my old bedside table, computer desk and chair, the radio alarm, the pictures on the walls had all miraculously appeared. It was as if someone had crept in during the early hours and installed a few things from my former life, just to make me feel more at home — but I knew that was patently ridiculous. Pushing the covers aside, I got out of bed and walked around, picking up objects which were undoubtedly my own personal possessions — a snow globe (a gift from Michelle), a gold-plated fountain pen (first prize in a junior school spelling competition), a pinewood bookcase crammed with my most beloved novels and biographies — things I hadn't seen in weeks.

Laid out on the desk, beside an artist's pencil, was a charcoal sketch of a horned owl, in such a way as to suggest that whoever had drawn the picture had done so recently. Leaning over, I scrutinised the initials in the bottom corner: NB.

"What?"

Disturbed, dumbfounded, I sat on the edge of the bed, muttering under my breath, wringing my hands, trying to work out what had happened, trying to go back over events in my mind. The last thing I remembered was the photograph of the horned owl tattoo, Michelle's wrist, and the unmistakable birthmarks. Then...then nothing.

Only when the radio alarm crackled into life did I get to my feet, walk, almost like an automaton, over to the sink, splash some cold water onto my face, and begin to dress.

Ten to fifteen minutes later, two knocks sounded against the door.

"Are you decent, Nige?"

I didn't answer.

Regardless, a key scraped around the lock, the deadbolt lowered, the door opened, and in walked Michael, a leather attaché case wedged under his arm. "Sorry I'm a little late, got caught in the most atrocious traffic jam."

"What – What are you doing here?"

He chuckled and gave me one of those light, facetious looks, as if I'd just made a reasonably amusing joke.

"Big day today, Nige." He pulled out the chair, turned it around, and was about to sit down, but stopped halfway, leaned over the desk and picked up the picture of the horned owl. He looked across at me. "Another owl picture? Do you think that's really wise?"

"How do you mean?" I asked, confused, flustered, not quite believing what was happening, what it all meant. All I knew was that his words made me feel defensive, so I blurted out: "I didn't do it. Someone shoved it under the door last night."

Slowly, carefully, he put the picture back on the desk, stood, straightened and looked at me very seriously, more seriously than I can ever remember him looking at me before.

"Nigel, listen, today some very important people are going to make some big decisions regarding your future."

"What? Another appraisal, you mean?"

"Yeah, an appraisal, if that's the way you want to look at it." He came closer and patted my shoulder. "After everything that's happened these last few weeks, all the trouble with the police, everything you've been through, I don't want to get your hopes up. Things might not go our way. Worst case scenario: you could be back here permanently, with no hope of another flat in a secure housing unit, a job placement, no hope of getting back into society, for at least the next three years."

"Three years," I repeated, remembering my solicitor's warning.

Michael checked his watch.

"Right, we've got five minutes to go through a few things." He sat down on the chair and gestured for me to do likewise, on the edge of the bed. "So you feel better now, yeah? Now you're back on your normal medication?"

I hesitated before saying, "Erm, yes," even though I had no idea what he was talking about. "I – I think so. Although I didn't realise I'd had any change to my usual prescription."

"And you haven't – not really. Only you keep forgetting to take it, don't you? So Doctor Forbes-Powers has upped the dosage, just until you're back on an even keel."

"Doctor Forbes-Powers? But—"

"That's right," Michael talked over me. "Now, in all, there's going to be five people on the panel. You're going to have to sit in front of them and answer all their questions, okay? In all likelihood, they'll try and ascertain your state of mind, whether or not you still present a danger to yourself. In all likelihood, the questions will be harsh, pointed, regarding your medication, the way you see yourself in the world, and how you interact with others, especially women."

"Wait," I said, almost shouted, in fact. "Who are you?"

"I'm your court-appointed psychiatric evaluator, Nige, but we don't look at things like that, do we? We're a team." He stood up and checked his watch again. "Come on, let's go. And remember to speak clearly at all times, don't lose your temper, try not dredge up the past – the future is what we're concerned about now, right?" He looked at me very seriously again. "And most importantly of all, at no point are you to mention the horned owl. Okay?"

I nodded and followed him out of the room.

But once we were in the corridor, I again had no idea where I was – or, more correctly, I did know where I was; only things didn't look quite the same. This corridor was like the corridor outside my office at the council building, but it led off into a room I'd never seen before. But, again, that wasn't strictly true, because this room – open-plan, a dozen or so plastic-backed chairs set out in a horseshoe formation, behind them two sofas, a coffee table – looked exactly like the room Doctor Rabie used for his counselling sessions.

"Hang on." I tugged at Michael's jacket. "Where are we going?"

He turned around. "I told you, to the, erm…appraisal, to talk about the future."

"Oh, right, yes, of course." I followed after him again. It was then I saw Liz, sitting on one of the sofas, alone, head lowered, as if she'd dozed off to sleep. And I felt such a joyous rush of emotion, I couldn't control myself.

"Liz! Liz!" I broke away from Michael, waving my arms in the air.

"Nigel! No!" He tried to grab me, but I slipped out of his grasp and rushed over to Liz. Only she didn't respond at all, she didn't even lift her head. It was as she was heavily sedated, as if she wasn't really there.

"Liz!" I knelt and took hold of her hands, which were warm and clammy to the touch. I looked up into her face, but her eyes were closed, as if she really was sleeping. To try and wake her, I shook and prodded her, hoping she'd open her eyes and speak to me. "Liz! I thought you were dead. I thought I'd never see you again."

The impact of this strangely stunted reunion was too much for me to take. I broke down in tears, burying my face in her lifeless lap.

"Come on, Nigel," said Michael. "We haven't got time for this."

As he pulled me to my feet, I caught a glimpse of a plastic box with an owl design on the lid. It was on the table, half open, only inside wasn't any velvet lining or shiny dagger but crayons, the colourful kind children used to draw with.

"Liz!" I shouted, almost beside myself. "Liz! It's me. Wake up. We can be together forever."

"Nigel, please! That isn't Liz, but your friend, Michelle. She suffers from a rare brain condition, remember? She can't talk like the rest of us. When you were here previously, you used to read to her, tell her stories, talk to her, sometimes you even made her smile."

By this time, I was almost hysterical, so much so, Michael had to slap me around the face. The jolt of which went some way to returning me to the here and now.

As I took the deep breaths Michael advised me to take, a smartly dressed young woman wearing a pair of tortoiseshell glasses crept into my peripheral vision.

"Is he all right?" she said to Michael.

Blinking away the tears, I turned and stared at her. And I had to do a complete double take – it was Helen King, only the name-tag fastened to her blouse didn't say Helen King but Liz Green.

"Yeah, yeah, he'll be fine. Nerves, I guess." He turned back to me. "Calm down, hey, Nige? You don't want to go up in front of the panel all flustered and emotional now, do you?"

"But, Liz, she's...Michelle...but you're called..."

Liz/Helen gave my forearm a reassuring squeeze.

"You're all confused, Nigel. Try and focus, clear your head. You were making such good progress before. Don't let it all go to waste, eh?"

"Come on, Nige," said Michael, slipping his arm through mine. "Let's go and speak to the board."

"No, no," I mumbled, trying to shake myself out of this delusion, this nightmare. "I'm not required to attend. My solicitor told me that before I was transferred here."

"Of course you're expected to attend," Michael leaned close and whispered. "In half-hour or so, it will all be over, everything will be decided."

We walked along the corridor, stopping outside a wooden door with a slim glass panel. Nigel knocked twice and we went inside.

The room was so brightly-lit I had difficulty focusing. Initially, therefore, all I could really make out was a long table, sat behind it, a mishmash of blurred human faces, suits, ties, a water jug, and stacks of files.

"Oh good," said a male voice I yet again recognised. "You're here. Please, Mr Oliver, Mr Barrowman, take a seat."

As Michael directed me to a chair, right in front of the panel, my vision finally levelled out, adjusted, and I could clearly make out everyone sitting before me. From right to left, each had a nameplate in front of them: Jeffrey Fuller, John Mackintosh, Julian Price, Gideon Forbes-Powers and Graham Bannister. But none of the faces staring back at me corresponded to the names on the nameplates – Jeffrey Fuller was Detective Inspector Watson, John Mackintosh was Gideon Forbes-Powers (the empty sleeve pinned to his lapel, where his left arm should have been only confirmed this), Julian Price was John Mackintosh, Gideon-Forbes-Powers was Detective Kendrick, and Graham Bannister was Doctor Rabie.

"Thank you for coming today," said Mackintosh. "If everyone is in agreement, I think we should progress straight to the heart of the matter." He turned the page of a thick file. Each member of the panel did likewise. "You know why you're here, don't you, Mr Barrowman?"

"Yes," I heard myself say.

"Two months ago, you sat before us in very different circumstances. You had responded well to all facets of your treatment. Twice-weekly, you had been travelling, on your own, to the council offices in Ilford, on an employment placement programme. Such was the quality of your work, the esteem in which you were held by your colleagues, the personnel section was more than happy to offer you full-time employment on a probationary basis. When secure housing informed us that a self-contained flat had become available, walking distance from your potential place of new employ, we decided it was time for you to try and reenter society." He looked up from the file. "You were getting on so well. What went wrong?"

All the time he was talking, I tried to follow the

chronological chain of events – but I couldn't, because I had a completely different memory of each metaphorical link.

"But – But I'd been working for the council for eight years."

This seemed to disturb the members of the panel. They each shifted position slightly and shared what I took for doubtful, concerned glances out of the corner of their eyes.

"No, no, Mr Barrowman," said Graham Bannister, "you've been in the mental health care system for eight years, ever since your breakdown. Don't you remember?"

To have said I didn't remember (which I didn't) was clearly the worst thing I could've said, like a confession, an acknowledgement of my inability to think straight, to function.

"Well, yes, of course…." I trailed off, hoping that would be enough to satisfy them.

"Eight years ago," said Julian Price, "you and your long-term partner, Riordan, decided to go your separate ways. You didn't take this very well at all. In the months following the end of the relationship, you rarely left your flat, you composed a lot of malicious letters, you dropped out of society altogether, you lost your job, you stopped eating, you drank heavily, took drugs, and, for the want of a better expression, engaged the services of many sex workers, both male and female, you started to self-harm. All of which culminated in a suicide attempt." He took a sip of water. "When you were eventually sectioned under the Mental Health Act, you were sent here for evaluation."

He turned and nodded to Doctor Rabie.

"When you first came under my care, Mr Barrowman," he said, "you had difficulty distinguishing between what was real and what was not – you were delusional. You claimed that you had been abused as a child, and that the abusers were Members of Parliament, the Establishment, High Court judges. You claimed that your life was at risk, that the shadow of death hung over you, that you were being pursued by a horned owl. To stabilise your mood, we put you on some anti-psychotic medication – which did indeed provide some essential ballast, as it were.

"However, the mental trauma you suffered in the months following the breakdown of your relationship proved deep-rooted. Moreover, the guilt you felt over your questionable sexual dalliances during this period affected you profoundly. Put simply: you didn't respond to conventional treatments."

"That's where I came in," said Gideon Forbes-Powers. "We decided to take a more holistic approach, encouraging you to take part in a creative writing programme. With something to focus your mind on, a disciplined routine, getting up each morning to write, you slowly began to regain your mental equilibrium." He too paused for a sip of water. "That the story you wrote had a strong homo-erotic theme only underpinned this, because it showed that you were exorcizing your demons, channelling all that negative energy, salving your guilt through the written word."

"*The Magister's Analects*, you mean?"

"That's correct," he said. "A powerful piece of writing, where you confront issues of social isolation, a person's need for warmth and intimacy in life. Granted, you suffered many set-backs along the way. You became quiet and withdrawn. But, eventually, when you'd gone through the whole process, we felt you were ready to move on to the next level."

Mackintosh was next to speak.

"Now, Mr Barrowman, I must repeat my earlier question: what, in your opinion, what, to the best of your knowledge, went wrong?" He didn't wait for an answer. Not that I would have been able to provide one, so dizzied and disturbed had I been by everything I'd just heard. "Firstly, we had the incident with the woman in the supermarket, the elderly lady you allegedly pushed to the floor, then accosted at a bus-stop. Giving you the benefit of the doubt, and having Doctor Bannister call round to the secure housing unit to question you, we decided to let you continue with your work duties and everyday life, on the condition that you call in to see Doctor Price at his Stratford clinic, once a fortnight.

"Next thing we hear you had absconded from your new flat, and hadn't turned up for work for over a week. We were worried. We reported you as a missing person. Imagine our surprise and disappointment when you were found sleeping rough in the basement of a squat, a derelict house, not five minutes walk from your nice, clean, well-appointed living space. Imagine our surprise and disappointment when we realised that you hadn't been taking your medication, that you had slipped back down the old delusional slope. Imagine our surprise and disappointment when you returned here and started to regurgitate your former abuse claims, when you spent every waking minute drawing pictures of a horned owl, when you tried to convince us of yet another murder plot against you and all other patients at the facility. Imagine our outright dismay when you stole some matches from the kitchen and attempted to set light to the recreation room."

"W – What?" I stammered. "But I…"

"Now, with all this in mind," said Mackintosh, "there is no way, in good conscience, that we can do anything other than recommend that you are once again interned here on a full-time basis."

"In the circumstances," said Michael, interceding for the first time, "we feel that is more than fair, and will not contest your decision. However, I would like to make an appeal on behalf of my client regarding the review period. As the panel today attested, Mr Barrowman has, in the past, responded well to treatment. If he sticks to his prescribed medication, he is more than able to function in society, to hold down a job, to look after himself. What I would like to suggest, therefore, would be a twelve-month review period, not the full three years that was suggested in our preliminary discussions."

The panel took a moment to confer, whispering amongst themselves.

"In principal," Mackintosh then said, "we have no objection to keeping the review period, how shall we say:

fluid, as it were. However, this will be determined by Mr Barrowman's willingness to undertake a different form of treatment."

"A different form of treatment?" Michael spoke for me.

"Yes," said Mackintosh. "On reviewing Mr Barrowman's case history, we feel it may be of benefit for him to undergo an extensive course of hypnotherapy."

It was then I knew what this was all about. It was then I knew why I'd felt so baffled and confused, why every face had a different name, every room a different appearance, every thought a different interpretation. It was then I remembered the words from Jane's journal, the stark warning about having our memories erased. It was then I knew that everything around me was a lie, a cover-up, that these people had got inside my head, and that I would never, ever be able to think straight again.

THE END

Fantastic Books
Great Authors

CROOKED CAT

Meet our authors and discover our exciting range:

- Gripping Thrillers
- Cosy Mysteries
- Romantic Chick-Lit
- Fascinating Historicals
- Exciting Fantasy
- Young Adult and Children's Adventures

Visit us at:
www.crookedcatbooks.com

Join us on facebook:
www.facebook.com/realcrookedcat

Printed in Great Britain
by Amazon